K

Gunsmoke Gold

GUNSMOKE GOLD

Gene Tuttle

AVALON BOOKS
THOMAS BOUREGY AND COMPANY, INC.
NEW YORK

DNU CT

PRINTED IN THE UNITED STATES OF AMERICA
BY HADDON CRAFTSMEN, SCRANTON, PENNSYLVANIA

Gunsmoke Gold

CHAPTER ONE

"Whoa, Nellie!" screamed Buster Gavin as he pulled back the reins of the stage team, his right foot slamming down on the brake shoe. The action nearly knocked his hat off, but he paid no mind to it. His full attention was focused on the lone figure standing beside the road, a rifle in his hands, a red bandana covering the bottom part of his face, while the lowered brim of his brown hat covered most of the top part.

The old stage rocked and twisted, nearly going off the winding dirt road, but Buster managed to stop it without any mishap. It was a good thing he hadn't been traveling too fast on the rough road along the edge of Windy Canyon.

"Hold still!" snapped the masked man as he moved closer to the stage and looked up at Buster.

"Whatcha lookin' for?" asked Buster. "We're clean as a whistle."

"Yeah?" grunted the masked man. "Where's the strongbox?"

"Back in Custer," replied Buster. "Nothin' to put in it."

The masked man grunted, moved over to the stage door, swung it open, and peered inside. But it was empty, so he slammed the door shut and walked around to the rear of the stage and looked at the boot. It was empty, too, except for the canvas covering which was rolled up and tied down.

Satisfied that there was nothing on the stage, the masked man turned and disappeared into the brush.

"I'll be darned!" grunted Buster as he started to pick up the reins. Then he stopped, shook his head, and glanced backward. "Maybe I'm crazy, but I sure had a passenger when I left Custer. Did he vamoose into thin air?"

He tied the reins to the railing on the seat and climbed down to the ground. Scratching his head thoughtfully, he opened the door. The stage was empty.

"I'll be darned!" he snorted.

Just then the door at the other side of the stage slowly opened and a young man's head peered around the edge at Buster.

"Whatcha doin' out there?" asked Buster.

"Is—is he gone?" asked the young man. "I heard him

and slipped out this door and crouched down, holding onto the door handle and keeping my feet on the step."

"Well, I'll be darned!" grunted Buster, shoving his hat way back on his head. "Well, climb in. He's pulled out. Hey, maybe you'd like to ride up on top with me?"

"That would be good," nodded the man. "It's very lonesome inside that bouncing stage."

"Come around here an' I'll help you up."

The young man closed the stage door and came around the stage as Buster closed the other door. Then the old-timer helped the young man up the front wheel and onto the wide driver's seat.

After they were moving again, the young man said, "I don't know how you felt, but I thought that gentleman would kill us both."

"First off, son, that wasn't a gentleman! Secondly, all he was lookin' for was money. Prob'ly didn't have enough nerve to pull that trigger."

"Well, I don't know about that. Anyway, I wasn't going to take any chances with him."

Buster eyed the young man. He was dressed in a nice-fitting brown suit, white shirt, and a necktie. On his feet were polished tan oxfords. He was about five foot ten and weighed possibly one hundred eighty. His brown hair was wavy and his brown eyes watched the scenery with great interest. Buster decided that this young man certainly was not from the cow country.

The young man noticed Buster's appraisal of him and he grinned widely.

"Lost my hat on the train when I was getting off and I

left my suitcase at the depot. When I got to the stage office, you were ready to pull out, so I forgot it until a while ago."

"Yeah, I noticed you didn't have a hat or suitcase," said Buster. "Just where are you from and what do you expect to do in Flat Bottom?"

"Well, I was working as a drummer in San Francisco when I got a letter from my uncle asking me to come and live with him," replied the young man. "I was alone, so I decided to come over here. Especially since I hated that job."

"I see," nodded Buster. "Who's your uncle?"

"Jim Benson."

Buster squinted at the young man, then shook his head.

"I'll be darned!" he grunted. "Jim Benson, eh? Didn't you know about Jim?"

"Know what?" the young man asked anxiously.

"He was shot a week ago. He's still unconscious at the doctor's house in Flat Bottom. Dunno if he'll pull through or not."

"Oh, no!" gasped the young man. "That's awful! Why was he shot?"

"That's a good question," grunted Buster. "Sheriff's been cuffin' his hat for a week tryin' to get an answer to that question."

"How did it happen?"

"No one seems to know," replied Buster. "Jim left the ranch ridin' into town, but he never got there. Two cowboys found him about a mile from town in the middle of the road, shot through the left shoulder. Doc said the bullet just missed his heart."

"That's terrible!" groaned the young man. "Do they shoot people often down here?"

"Aw, just now an' then," replied Buster.

"What about holding up the stage?"

"Oh, sometimes they'll do that when the payroll for the Golden Eagle Mine's due to come through from the bank in Custer." Buster paused and chuckled. "That varmint behind that mask sure was surprised when he didn't find anythin'."

"I have a strong feeling that I'm not going to like it here," sighed the young man.

"It grows on you. Look at me. Came here forty years ago for a spell an' I'm still here. Say, I don't know your handle." He saw that the young man looked puzzled. "Your name."

"I'm Peter Benson. And what's your handle?"

"Glad to meetcha, Pete. I'm Buster Gavin, stage driver deluxe."

Peter nodded just as they reached the top of a mesa. "What's that ahead of us, Buster?"

The driver squinted and began to slow down the stage.

"I'll be darned!" he grunted, coming to a stop. "It looks like someone's hurt."

Two bodies were sprawled in the middle of the road.

"Holy hen hocks!" gasped Buster as he jumped to the ground. "This ain't good, Pete!"

Peter jumped down while Buster knelt next to the bodies, looking closely at them.

"I'll be darned!" the driver grunted. "Charley King

an' Fred Hansen! They left Custer 'bout an hour before we did."

"What happened to them?" asked Peter.

"Without any crystal ball, I reckon someone shot both of 'em. They're dead as can be," replied Buster, getting to his feet and brushing off the knees of his Levi's. He sighed deeply. "Just a while ago, they was alive. Now look! Nothin' we can do, so we better fetch the sheriff an' coroner."

"Where are they?"

"I hope they're in Flat Bottom. C'mon, Pete."

They both climbed up on the seat, and Buster turned to the young man. "Just hold on tight, Pete, 'cause I'm goin' to make this real fast." He slapped the reins over the four-horse team, which broke into a gallop.

A little later, as they neared town, the old-timer said, "See down there. That's Flat Bottom."

Peter could see a small settlement in the center of a fertile valley.

Right next to the town ran a wide river with willows on both sides.

"I'll be glad to get there," said Peter, holding onto the railing with his left hand while his right hand held tight to the edge of the seat.

"That's two of us," shouted Buster.

Flat Bottom was just that: flat as could be. The main street was a block and a half long, with false-fronted buildings badly in need of paint. Old-timers in this Arizona valley said that Indians had first called the place

Flat Bottom. And although many had wanted to change the name, they never did.

Since the discovery of gold at the Golden Eagle Mine on the north end of the valley, the little town had really perked up. There were four large cattle ranches in the valley, too. The Box B, owned by Jim Benson, was at the north end of the valley and east of the Bubbling River. Across the river in the middle of the valley, was the Lazy N, owned by Mike Nelson. The Circle H, which belonged to Grady Halstead, was at the south end of the valley and east of the river, and the Double D, owned by Clyde Duggan, was on the southwest end of the valley.

There was little activity on the main street before Buster stopped at the sheriff's office. But now people wondered why the stage driver wanted to see the lawman.

Deputy Harry Baylor stepped into the open doorway, then turned back and called out to the sheriff:

"Hey, Wilbur! Somethin's wrong. Stage just pulled up outside!"

Harry hurried out on the walk as Wilbur Wendell came to the doorway and looked at the scene. People were coming from different directions, rushing to the stage.

"What's the matter, Buster?" asked the sheriff. "Can't you talk?"

"That'd be new for Buster," remarked one of the crowd.

"Charley King an' Fred Hansen are dead," said the

stage driver, waving his right hand toward the road. "Just about two miles from here. On the mesa."

"Whoa, simmer down!" snapped the sheriff. "You say King an' Hansen are dead? How do you know?"

"How do I—oh, hell, you don't have to be a doctor to tell when someone's dead, Sheriff. Both of 'em shot in the back!"

"Who coulda done that?" grunted the deputy, scratching his head.

"That's for you to find out," snapped Buster. "Now I gotta report—hey, I plumb forgot! Masked man stopped the stage a few miles back from where we found them two dead men."

"What'd he get?" asked the sheriff.

"Nothin'—maybe indigestion," chuckled Buster. "This here young one is Peter Benson, nephew of ol' Jim's."

"Jim's nephew, eh?" said the sheriff. "Drop him off at Doc's and tell Doc to get his wagon and we'll meet him on the edge of town."

The sheriff turned and looked at Harry Baylor. "Don't just stand there. Act alive, Harry. Get our broncs pronto!"

"Uh-huh," nodded the deputy as he lumbered away.

The stage moved down the street and around the corner. The sheriff stood on the walk scratching his neck thoughtfully.

Wilbur Wendell, sixty, had been sheriff of Paradise County for eight years. He learned his stuff on the job, and everyone agreed that he was an efficient officer. But he was quite disturbed by the two murders.

* * *

Buster drew the stage up in front of the doctor's house, jumped down, and ran to the door. Peter Benson climbed down slowly and followed the old-timer. He got to the door just as Dr. Schulte appeared in response to Buster's loud knocking.

"Got two dead men, Doc!" snapped the driver.

"Out in the stage?" asked Doc.

"Hell, no! Out on the mesa. Sheriff said to get your wagon an' meet him on the edge of town. It's Charley King an' Fred Hansen."

"They're dead?" gasped Doc, a small, wiry man with a bushy mustache. "Both from the Golden Eagle Mine, aren't they?"

"Uh-huh, you got it right, Doc," nodded Buster. Then he gestured to Peter. "Doc, this is Peter Benson, nephew of ol' Jim Benson. How's Jim gettin' along?"

"Benson's nephew, eh? Jim's still holding his own. Come on in, son, and you can see the old man. He's unconscious, but you can see him. My wife's in there with him."

Buster went back to the stage, climbed up, and slowly drove around the back of town to the livery stable where the stage office was also located. He pulled into the stable and climbed down as Emory Hill, stage agent, and Neal Thompson of the Golden Eagle came out to meet him.

"How was the trip?" asked Emory.

"Oh, yeah, you didn't hear yet, huh?"

"Hear what?" snapped Emory.

"We was held up an' then we—"

"What?" said Thompson. "You mean that someone stole the payroll?"

"Oh, no." Buster shook his head. "We foxed him. But a little way toward town we came across King an' Hansen—dead as a doorknob."

"You what?" gasped Thompson, grabbing Buster by the arm and shaking him. "What did you say?"

"You heard me, Thompson. We found King an' Hansen in the middle of the road, both shot in the back."

Thompson shook his head.

"I—I can't believe it," he said slowly. "Why, they was going over to Custer as a decoy on the payroll shipment."

"Someone musta thought they had it," said Emory as he followed Buster to the rear of the stage where the old man carefully unrolled the boot's canvas covering. Inside the canvas was the payroll for the Golden Eagle Mine, wrapped tightly in newspaper.

"Safe as a church. No one would ever think of lookin' here," said Buster.

Thompson came over and looked at the payroll.

"Charley an' Fred dead," he muttered. "I—I just can't believe it."

"The sheriff is headin' out there now," said Buster.

"I don't want to see them dead," Thompson said quietly as he picked up the payroll. "I'll take this to the mine, then ride back."

"Life is so blasted uncertain," Emory sighed.

CHAPTER TWO

Sheriff Wilbur Wendell and Deputy Harry Baylor rode a fair distance ahead of Doc Schulte as they left town. When they reached the bodies, the lawmen were surprised to see two cowboys standing nearby, their horses off the road, reins dragging. The cowboys looked at the two officers, the sunlight glistening on their badges.

"Glad to see the law here," the taller cowboy said. "We just rode in on this mess."

Wilbur Wendell nodded as he climbed laboriously down from his saddle. Harry Baylor climbed down easily. The two officers looked curiously at the two men, then at the sprawled bodies.

11

"When did you two get here?" asked the sheriff.

"Probably ten minutes ago," replied the shorter cowboy. "Sorry I don't carry a watch to let you know exactly when, Sheriff."

"Huh!" grunted the sheriff as he stepped gingerly around the corpses, looking closely at them.

Harry stood still and glanced around. "Wonder where their horses are," he said.

"We didn't see any horses," replied the taller cowboy. "I'm sure they weren't on foot, though."

The sheriff looked at his deputy.

"Buster never mentioned horses, either," he said.

"They must have been on horses," said the taller cowboy.

The sheriff squinted thoughtfully at him and slowly nodded.

"Horses prob'ly took off at the shootin'," he said. "Where did you two come from?"

"Last big town was Custer," replied the shorter cowboy. "This is the road to Flat Bottom, isn't it?"

"It is," nodded Harry Baylor. "Over this mesa and down into the valley."

The sheriff walked slowly around the two bodies while the others watched him. He paused several times, looking at the dead men from different angles.

The taller cowboy moved over and pointed at one of the bodies.

"This fellow was shot first," he said.

"Was, huh?" grunted the sheriff, looking closely at the body, then up at the tall cowboy. "How do you figure that one out, stranger?"

"Just look at the two bodies," said the cowboy. "This one still has his gun in his holster, but the other one doesn't."

"That don't tell me nothin'," grunted the sheriff. "Could have fallen out of his holster."

"It could have, but I'm willing to bet that it didn't," said the taller cowboy. "Doesn't it strike you as funny that they should be side by side on the road?"

The sheriff glanced at his deputy, then back to the cowboy.

"I don't get your reasonin'."

"How could they both have been shot in the back— while riding their horses—and fallen off side by side?" asked the cowboy. "It doesn't make sense to me."

"Doesn't, huh?" said the sheriff, shaking his head. "Yeah, it doesn't—does it?"

"You mean someone, after shootin' 'em, dragged 'em out here in the middle of the road an' left 'em?" asked Harry Baylor, rubbing his chin thoughtfully.

"That's the idea, Deputy," said the taller cowboy. "Of course, they could have been shot somewhere else and brought here, too."

"The more you talk, the deeper this thing seems," groaned the sheriff as he shook his head.

Just then Doc Schulte drew near with his wagon and team. While he stepped down and walked toward the two bodies, the taller cowboy turned to Wilbur Wendell.

"You know these two gents, Sheriff?"

The sheriff nodded. "Charley King, with the gun in his holster, an' one of his pardners, Fred Hansen, of the Golden Eagle Mine. And I'm Sheriff Wilbur Wendell, an' this deputy is Harry Baylor." He pointed to the doctor. "That's Doc Schulte."

As they began shaking hands, the taller cowboy said:

"I'm Silent Slade and this is my partner, Irish O'Day."

After the formality was over, Doc squatted on his heels beside the bodies and looked grimly at them. Then he got slowly to his feet, shaking his head.

"Terrible way to leave this earth," he said and took two big blankets from his wagon. "Know anything about it, Sheriff?"

"Only what Buster told me when he drove into town."

Silent helped the doctor spread the blankets out on the ground beside the bodies. Next he helped Doc lift the bodies onto the blankets.

It was then that the two officers and Irish moved forward to carry the corpses, one at a time, to the wagon where they were placed side by side.

"Thank you kindly," said Doc Schulte as he climbed into the wagon.

"You can follow Doc to Flat Bottom," said the sheriff when the wagon drove off.

"You're not going there?" asked Silent.

"We're goin' to look around a little before headin' for town," replied the sheriff.

"Mind if we stay a spell and help you look?" asked Silent. "You know, eight eyes are better'n four."

The sheriff smiled and nodded.

"Glad to have all the help we can get," he said. "Things like this kinda make me confused. I hate murders—an' here we got two."

"An' don't forget the stage," said Harry.

"Stage?" Silent asked. "What about the stage?"

Irish grinned as he watched his partner. He knew that these murders would set Silent's brain into motion.

"Oh, the stage driver reported that a masked man held him up a ways back from here toward Custer, but he got nothin' an' left in a hurry," replied the sheriff. "Mighty funny situation."

"It certainly is," agreed Silent. "Held up the stage, got nothing, and took off—and then the stage driver found the bodies."

"You don't think the two things could be tied together in any way, do you?" Irish asked curiously.

The sheriff slowly thought it over. "Yeah." He nodded his head. "It could be. Maybe. The stage usually brings the Golden Eagle payroll into Flat Bottom."

"And the two men murdered were working at the mine?" asked Silent.

"Charley King owned a small share and was the bookkeeper for the mine, and Fred Hansen was also part owner," replied the sheriff.

"The killer was probably looking for the payroll," said Silent. "They tried to cover all possibilities."

"Buster said it was just one masked man," Harry said.

"Yeah," nodded Silent. "One man could have done it, then took their horses after finding they didn't have the payroll on themselves. Maybe the horses carried the payroll."

"Hey, I never thought of that," said the sheriff.

"Reckon we better head back to Flat Bottom an' talk with Buster an' that young fellow that came in with him."

"Good idea," Harry said. "Goin' to be dark soon, an' after this, I kinda hate ridin' in the dark."

Peter Benson sat next to his uncle's bed. He studied Jim Benson's wrinkled face. He had never seen the old man before, and it was like looking at a stranger.

When Mrs. Schulte came in to check on the patient, she smiled at Peter. Then she brought him a cup of coffee and several cookies, and gave him a few encouraging words. As it started to get dark outside, she brought in an oil lamp, and Uncle Jim grunted and spat. She looked down at the man.

Suddenly he opened his eyes and glanced at Peter and the woman. Then he closed his eyes and groaned loudly.

"Uncle Jim, it's me, Peter," said the young man, peering closely at the old-timer.

Mrs. Schulte put a hand on Peter's shoulder. He glanced up at her, then back to his uncle. They both watched the man intently.

A minute or two later, Jim Benson again opened his eyes and looked curiously at them. Peter spoke his name, but it didn't seem to register with the old man. This time he blinked several times and slowly licked his dry lips with his tongue.

"Would you like some water?" asked Mrs. Schulte.

There was no indication that he heard anything. He just looked around, groaning sharply. Suddenly he jerked up in bed as though someone had lifted his shoulders. His face twisted in pain.

Before either of them could do anything, the old man slumped back on the pillow, his head rolling to one side, his eyes closed. His face seemed to relax.

"He's dead," said Mrs. Schulte softly.

"Are you sure?" Peter asked.

She nodded. "I've seen it many times, Peter." Then she slowly drew the sheet and blanket up over the still form. "We better go into the front room and wait for Doc."

Peter got to his feet, glancing back at the covered figure. Then he followed the woman out of the room. She closed the door quietly and they went to the front room. Peter sank down on the sofa, shaking his head and sighing deeply.

"I—I never had a chance to talk with him," he said slowly. "What a sad day this has been for me."

"You've been broken into Arizona the hard way," said Mrs. Schulte. "I'll fix us some fresh coffee as we wait for Doc."

"I certainly appreciate your kindness," Peter said. "Just think, I came all the way here to this."

"Did he have any other relatives?"

"I doubt it," replied Peter. "In his letter he said I was his only living relative."

"Then you'll probably inherit the Box B ranch," said the woman. "It's one of the biggest in this part of the state."

"I don't care about that." Peter shook his head. "I just wish Uncle Jim were still alive."

"I know how you must feel," said the woman sympathetically. "I'll get that coffee and some more cookies."

As she started for the kitchen, there was a knock on the front door, so she opened it. Two cowboys were standing in the doorway. They took off their dusty hats and smiled at her.

"Howdy, Mrs. Schulte," said the younger of the two.

"Oh, Dale, Ike, I'm glad to see you." She paused and shook her head sadly. "But Jim's dead."

The two cowboys stood there motionless, looking shocked. Finally the first one shook his head.

"It just had to come," he said. "When did it happen?"

"Just a few minutes ago," replied Mrs. Schulte. "Come in."

They slowly moved into the front room, leaving the door wide open. They stopped, looking curiously at Peter.

"This is Peter Benson," explained Mrs. Schulte. "He was with his uncle when he died."

"Peter Benson?" asked the first cowboy. "You don't mean you're Jim's nephew?"

Peter got to his feet, nodding his head and holding out his right hand.

"I'm Dale Boyd, ramrod for Jim, an' this talkin' machine with me is Ike Jones." The three shook hands, but there was little enthusiasm in their gestures.

"I got here too late," said Peter. "He woke up, but I doubt if he knew anything. This is terrible."

Mrs. Schulte quickly told Dale and Ike what Peter had encountered on his first day in Arizona.

"You gotta live with it," said Ike. "I know it's hard on

you, but life must go on. And in my forty years, I've seen lotsa life."

"That's right," nodded Dale. "Life's gotta go on. But Jim was lookin' forward to your comin' here. He told us that you'd take over the ranch after he died." He paused and looked at Mrs. Schulte. "Where's Doc?"

"He had to go out to bring in the two bodies," replied Mrs. Schulte. "The ones Peter saw today!"

"Yes, I saw them," Peter said. "It was awful. I think their names are King and Hansen. They're from some mine."

"Charley King an' Fred Hansen?" Dale said. "Are you sure about that?"

Peter nodded. "That's who the stage driver said they were."

Dale and Ike exchanged glances.

"Why, they were at the ranch last night sayin' they was goin' to ride over to Custer," said Ike. "What's goin' to happen to the Golden Eagle now?"

"Three of the pardners dead," sighed Dale. "It's hard to believe."

"Who was the third one?" asked Peter.

"Your uncle owned thirty-five percent of the mine," Dale said. "He an' Hansen were the big owners. King, I believe, had ten percent and Neal Thompson had the remainin' twenty percent."

"You mean Uncle Jim invested in mining, too?" asked Peter.

"He invested in anythin' he thought would make money," replied Dale. "I don't know just what he owned here in town, but I'll bet he owned an interest in many different businesses."

At that moment a sound outside caused them to look through the open doorway. Doc Schulte had just drawn up in front with his wagon and the two bodies. There were curious people surrounding the wagon. Doc climbed down from the seat and shoved his way to the front door.

"Jim Benson's dead," said Mrs. Schulte.

Doc shook his head.

"They always say it runs in threes," he sighed. "I've got to have some help placing the bodies in the work shed out back."

"We'll help you, Doc," offered Dale. "C'mon, Ike."

Peter stood in the doorway a moment and watched as Doc selected some of the men from outside to help, too. They carried the bodies around the house. Then Mrs. Schulte had Peter come in and sit down.

"He'll be back in a minute," she said.

"Things seem to become more confused every minute," sighed Peter.

"That's the way it is here," said the woman.

Silent Slade, Irish O'Day, Sheriff Wilbur Wendell, and Deputy Harry Baylor swung their horses into the main street of Flat Bottom as the sun dipped down, casting long, weird purple shadows across the town.

"So this is Flat Bottom, eh?" said Irish as they stopped in front of the sheriff's office and dismounted.

"It's a mighty nice place," said Harry. "It grows on you."

"I reckon it would have to," laughed Irish. "I was curious about the place when I learned the name because I have never seen a flat bottom. They're always rounded."

The men all laughed as Silent and Irish took their war sacks off their saddles and headed for the hotel, which was two doors away from the sheriff's office. They were given a nice upstairs room with a big window that opened onto the balcony.

"This is probably the neatest hotel room I've seen in years," said Silent, sitting down on the edge of his bed, testing it. "Not bad for two bits a night."

"Everything's fine except that porch out there," complained Irish as he looked out the window. "Easy for anyone to get into our room without using the door."

"Expecting someone, partner?"

"You never know," replied Irish, turning away from the window. "We've had a taste of what goes on around here. Maybe we shouldn't have come here, Silent."

"Joe Fisher said it was a simple thing," said Silent, stretching out on his bed. "All he said was for us to come here and see Jim Benson."

"Uh-huh, but it's them simple things from Joe Fisher's Westland Cattlemen's Association that get so damn complicated," complained Irish. "And from the looks of it, we've ridden into somethin' that's not too simple."

"Funny thing, masked man holding up the stage and finding nothing," mused Silent. "Then those two corpses. Like some kind of riddle."

"And you're going to try and solve it, eh?"

Silent Slade lifted his head slightly and squinted at Irish. He knew that Irish always complained but was eager to get involved. For several years they had traveled together throughout the West, working for different cattlemen's associations and for private detective agencies. If that work was slack, they'd hitch on with some ranch for a few months. It seemed that both men had the urge to become involved in any kind of mystery. And they were ready to tackle many opponents, for they were big men.

Silent Slade was well over six feet tall. In fact, in his high-heeled boots and Stetson hat, he was closer to seven feet. His face was long and lean and bronzed. His cheekbones were prominent, his hair dark. His long nose was slightly out of line with the rest of his face. His gray eyes seemed to drill holes when he stared at anyone. Many had claimed that at times Silent Slade looked like the Devil. But when he smiled, his entire face changed.

Irish O'Day, slightly under six feet, was broad of shoulder and as strong as a bull. He was deeply tanned and his red hair stuck out beneath the brim of his hat. His cobalt-blue eyes always had an amazed expression in them. His mouth was a mere slit until he broke into a grin. Then it seemed to cover his entire face.

At one time Silent Slade had been known in many countries because of his acts of magic. When he was quite young, he ran away from home, joined a circus, and learned how to become a magician. But he tired of the circus life and eventually became a cowboy with a nose for trouble. He started out solo. Then he met Irish O'Day when they worked on the same ranch. Irish loved adventure and never backed down from any fight, so they teamed up and soon became a legend in the West.

"After we talk with Jim Benson, we'll know which direction to go in," said Silent.

"Yeah? I can tell you right now which direction we'll go. If anyone finds out we're here for the association, we'll be as welcome as a rattlesnake at a roadrunner's convention."

"Don't cross your bridges before they're built," cautioned Silent as he reached into his hip pocket and pulled out a deck of cards.

Irish sat down on the edge of the bed and watched Silent as he manipulated the cards into different designs. Then he took out two jacks from the deck and laid them face up on the bedspread beside him. He looked at them, then at Irish.

"Like those two corpses we rode in on," he said. "I'd like to know where they were shot and why they were dumped on the road like they were."

"Maybe they wanted the stage driver to find them," suggested Irish.

"Could be—but why?" Silent picked up the two jacks and shoved them into the deck.

"Pull out the answer," grinned Irish.

"I wish it was that easy," sighed Silent as he tapped the cards and shoved them back in his hip pocket. He often played card tricks on people, and Irish was awed by the tricks, no matter how often he watched them.

"Hey, you know, pardner, we haven't eaten since breakfast," reminded Irish. "I could eat the hind leg off a runnin' steer and pick my teeth with his horns."

CHAPTER THREE

Peter Benson sat in the lobby of the hotel in Flat Bottom and tried to think what he would do. He had looked forward to meeting his uncle, and now the old man was dead. Several people said that he would inherit everything his uncle possessed, but he wondered. It was too good to be true.

The flickering oil lamps around the lobby cast unusual shadows on the walls. Peter looked curiously at them, as if they could tell him something about his future. His train of thought was interrupted by the appearance of Silent Slade and Irish O'Day as they came back from their supper.

Peter looked at them and Silent grinned as he came over and quickly introduced himself and Irish.

"Strangers, too, eh?" said Peter. "Sit down and rest."

They sat down, Silent next to Peter on a sofa, while Irish drew up an old rocker in front of the two.

"Were you the young man in the stage this afternoon?" asked Silent.

Peter nodded. "It was me. Suppose everyone's heard about it by now."

"Not in Alaska as yet," grinned Irish.

"Mind telling me your version of everything?" asked Silent.

"I suppose you've heard it all, but I'll do the best I can," said Peter. Then he told them all about his stage ride.

"What a welcome to Arizona," grunted Irish. "If such a thing happened to me, I'd catch the first stage outa here."

"I've been thinking about doing just that," said Peter. "But I must stay here for a while until my uncle's estate is settled."

"Oh," said Silent. "Who was your uncle?"

"Jim Benson of the Box B ranch."

Silent and Irish exchanged quick glances. This was the man they had come to Flat Bottom to see.

"What happened to him?" asked Silent.

Peter explained what he knew.

Silent listened closely. "Then you never were able to talk with him, eh?" he asked.

"I talked, but he didn't know anything," Peter said, shaking his head sadly. "I'm sorry I took so long to get here."

"Does the law have any idea why he was shot?" asked Silent.

"I don't know," replied Peter. "I haven't really talked to the law here as yet."

"Oh, oh, you will now," said Irish quickly as he spotted the sheriff stepping into the hotel lobby.

Silent and Peter half turned and looked at the approaching law officer.

"Sheriff Wendell, this is Peter Benson," said Silent.

Wilbur nodded, pulled up a chair, and sat down. "We were sort of introduced earlier." He turned to Peter. "Too bad about your uncle," he said. "Knew him for years, and he was a great man."

"Then why was he murdered?" asked Silent.

The sheriff looked at Silent and shook his head.

"Yeah, it's murder now," he said. "I dunno why anyone would shoot Jim Benson. Everyone liked him. Never had an enemy."

"Sounds like a character out of a book," remarked Silent. "But there is a flaw in what you said, Sheriff. Someone didn't like him."

"There you go again," groaned the sheriff. He turned to Irish. "Is he like this all the time?"

"Like what?" asked Irish.

"Askin' questions that no one can answer," replied the sheriff. "I don't know what your business is, but I think I'm smart enough not to ask."

"Good reasoning, sheriff," said Silent.

The lawman turned to Peter again and asked him about the events of the day, so Peter told him everything he knew. When he finished, the sheriff sat back and sighed.

"One masked man, two dead bodies, an' now Jim Benson."

"Did Benson have any problems that you know of?" asked Silent.

"I just done told you about Jim Benson," replied the sheriff. "No, I don't think he had any problems at all."

Suddenly a tall, heavyset man came into the lobby and walked over to the four men. The sheriff looked curiously at him. Then he introduced Clay Bannister, attorney-at-law.

Bannister did not shake hands. He merely nodded and turned his attention to Peter Benson.

"You claim to be Peter Benson?" When Peter nodded, he continued, "I must have proof. I was Jim Benson's lawyer and I have his will. And he never once mentioned a Peter Benson."

Peter's face went white.

"I—I am Peter Benson. Have been ever since I was born. My father was Jim Benson's brother, Earl. I have a letter from my uncle asking me to come and live with him, and he said I was the only living relative he had."

Bannister shook his head.

"That's impossible," he said. "His will names an Annie Benson of Phoenix as his sole heir. Where's that letter of yours?"

"In my suitcase," replied Peter.

"Well, get it!" snapped the lawyer.

Peter started to get up, then dropped back down on the sofa.

"It's in my suitcase in Custer," he said. "Had to catch the stage and I got there as it was ready to leave, so I didn't go back for my suitcase."

"Huh!" grunted Bannister. "I'll need that letter right away."

"Won't tomorrow do?" asked Silent, taking a dislike to the lawyer.

Bannister thought it out, then nodded. "Yes, have it here tomorrow afternoon." He paused. "Why did you take the authority to tell the doctor not to have a funeral for Jim Benson?"

Peter looked bewildered, shaking his head.

"I—the doctor said Uncle told him that when he died he didn't want people looking at him, so we decided not to have a funeral but bury him in the morning. Oh, yes, two cowboys, Dale and Ike, said Uncle had told them that, too."

"Crazy!" snorted the attorney. "A prominent man like Jim Benson going to his final rest without any respect from his host of friends."

"I believe he was right," said Silent. "That's my request when I go."

"Well, I don't agree with you!" Bannister snapped, then turned to Peter again. "Get that letter to me before five o'clock."

With that he strode out of the lobby. Silent glanced at Peter, who looked like a whipped dog.

"Don't let him bluff you," said Silent. "His bark is worse than his bite."

"Bannister is a powerful man here," said the sheriff.

"Because he knows how to bluff people," said Silent.

"I hate attorneys who think they know it all. You can get that letter, Peter, can't you?"

Peter nodded. "I'll have to ride over to Custer in the morning on the stage and pick it up."

"Buster will get it for you," said the sheriff. "I'll ask him, so you won't have to ride over an' back."

"I'd certainly appreciate that," said Peter. "I don't care to ride in that stage."

"Well, I think we'll hit the hay," said Silent, stretching.

Peter got to his feet. He saw something on the floor and stooped down to pick it up when a gun was fired near the hotel doorway. The sheriff's hat went spinning before everyone hit the floor. Silent pushed Peter down flat. Then he rolled over, drawing his gun. He glanced around the sofa toward the door, saw no one, so he leaped to his feet and ran to the doorway. He looked out at the dark street.

"See anyone?" Irish asked as he joined his partner, gun in hand.

"Too dark," muttered Silent, moving out on the walk and looking around.

From the sheriff's office came Harry Baylor, running toward the hotel.

"What happened?" the deputy demanded.

"Someone took a shot at one of us," said Silent as he went back inside the lobby, followed by Irish and Harry.

"My gosh!" gasped the sheriff, holding up his hat with a bullet hole through the crown. "Who's tryin' to kill me?"

Silent shook his head.

"You must have done something to someone," he said.

Peter looked curiously at Silent, then at the sheriff.

The sheriff's hands trembled as he pushed his hat on his head and walked out of the lobby, followed by Harry.

"Let's retire before there's another shot," suggested Peter. "This has been a trying day for me."

They all went up the stairs to their rooms. Peter had the room across the hall from Silent and Irish.

"All right now," said Irish after he had locked the door and Silent had lighted the oil lamp on the dresser. "Why did someone shoot at the sheriff?"

"They didn't," replied Silent. "Peter was the target, but he stooped down to pick up something just as the gent fired, leaving the sheriff in the line of fire. Glad he shot high."

"Why didn't you tell the sheriff?" asked Irish. "The poor guy won't sleep a wink tonight worryin' over it."

"I hope he does worry," said Silent as he started to undress. "It just might put his think box into gear. He might find some answers to questions that have been bothering him."

First thing the next morning, Silent and Irish went to seek the sheriff and tell him what they knew, but they found Harry Baylor holding down the office. He greeted them.

"Takin' charge till Wilbur comes back," he said.

"Did he leave town?" asked Silent.

"Oh, no, he's out at the cemetery with Doc, Peter Benson, Dale, Ike, and Sody Smith, buryin' the old man," replied the deputy. "Thought it would be better if the law was present. Them fellows worked for Jim Benson for a long time."

Silent nodded. "Tell the sheriff that whoever fired that shot last night wasn't shooting at him."

"They wasn't, huh? Shucks, that'll bust his balloon. He's been paradin' around like a peacock thinkin' someone tried to kill him. But who was the bullet meant for?"

"Peter Benson," replied Silent as they walked out, leaving a very bewildered deputy behind them.

Silent and Irish were just finishing their breakfast in a small cafe next to the hotel when the sheriff came tramping in, followed by Peter, Dale, Ike, and Sody.

"What's this Harry told me?" asked the sheriff.

Silent nodded. "That bullet was intended for Peter Benson, but he stooped to pick up something from the floor, leaving you in line with the killer."

Peter's eyes widened and his mouth sagged. "But why would anyone want to kill me?"

"That's another question for the sheriff to file away," said Silent, moving his eyes toward the three Box B cowboys. "You boys from Benson's spread?"

Dale nodded. "I'm ramrod for the outfit. Name's Dale Boyd. This fella next to me is Ike Jones. The sourlookin' cuss is Sody Smith, ranch cook."

Silent introduced himself and Irish.

"Slade, huh?" grunted Dale, rubbing his chin thoughtfully. "That name rings a bell with me. Did I ever know you before?"

"I doubt that," Silent said, then turned to Peter. "Is the stage driver getting that suitcase in Custer?"

"Uh-huh. Buster's bringing it here this afternoon," said Peter. "But I'm not as much interested in the suitcase as I am in living. I don't like to have anyone shoot at me. I haven't done a thing to anyone here."

"None of us like to be shot at," said Irish. "Likely there's a reason behind someone shootin' at you."

"I haven't been here that long," said Peter.

"I think we better take him out to the ranch," suggested Dale. "That way we can kinda look after him."

"I'm for that," grunted the sheriff. "Get him outa my hair right now 'cause I've got too much to think about without dry-nursin' a tenderfoot."

The sheriff walked out. The other men sat down at a table near Silent and Irish.

Suddenly Dale stood up and walked over to Silent. "Joe Fisher sent you," he said softly. "Right?"

Silent looked up at him, then nodded. "Confidential," he said softly. "We'll ride out later and talk."

"Good," nodded Dale. "I knew that name rang a bell."

Silent and Irish finished their meal and walked out, taking a good look at the main street of Flat Bottom. There was very little activity. The only horses at the hitchrack belonged to the Box B. An old broken-down freight wagon with two mules was heading out of town.

"Let's rest on the hotel porch," suggested Irish. "It's shady and we can see the entire main street from there."

They watched the Box B boys with Peter come out of the cafe. Peter came up to the hotel. He went inside, then returned in a few minutes, while Ike came over with an extra saddle horse.

"I paid my room," Peter said to Silent. "I suppose it would be best for me to stay at the ranch until things settle down."

"We'll ride out after the stage comes in with your suitcase," said Silent.

"I'd certainly appreciate that."

"It's also a good excuse to get out to the Box B without attracting too much attention," Silent said.

Peter turned and joined the other men. Then they all rode out of town.

"Game young chump," said Irish. "If someone had taken a shot at me, I'd of left on that stage this morning."

"Funny about that lawyer saying that some gal would inherit the Box B," said Silent.

"Yeah, that's queer when Peter said his uncle wrote him that he was the only living relative. Do you smell something', cowboy?"

"Uh-huh, a skunk."

Silent and Irish were walking out of the cafe when the stage drew up in front of the sheriff's office. They hurried over there as the sheriff and deputy came out on the walk.

"Stopped again!" snapped Buster. "I'll be damned— yes, I will!"

"What happened?" demanded the sheriff.

"Masked man. Think it was the same one as yesterday."

"What'd he take?"

"That tenderfoot's suitcase, that's all," replied Buster.

"Happened about where we found them bodies yesterday."

Silent looked curiously at Irish. Then they edged out of the crowd and went through the hotel lobby and out the rear to an alley that led to the livery stable where they quickly saddled their horses. They headed out of town just as the stage came to the livery stable.

"Whatcha make of it, cowboy?" asked Irish as they rode north on the road that led to the Golden Eagle Mine and the Box B ranch.

"Cinch someone doesn't want Peter to get that ranch."

They rode in silence then. Finally they saw a sign with the Box B brand on it.

"Maybe Dale Boyd can be helpful," said Silent as they cantered over a slight rise, getting a view of the ranch house, the large stable with corrals on either side, and the bunkhouse.

They dismounted in front of the main house when the door opened. Peter came out on the porch, followed by Sody Smith, carrying a shotgun.

"Howdy," greeted Silent as he eyed the old cook. "Expecting trouble?"

"Never take a chance," said Sody as he lowered the shotgun. "Come in outa the sun an' rest your bunions."

Peter looked closely at the two men.

"Where's my suitcase?" he asked.

"It didn't make it to Flat Bottom," said Silent. "That masked man stopped the stage and took it with him."

"Why would he take my suitcase?" asked Peter.

"Maybe he wanted to read that letter from your

uncle," Irish suggested.

"Yes, that letter." Peter paused. "Oh, I've got to have it to show that lawyer this afternoon."

"I'm afraid you won't have it to show him," said Silent. "Tell me, where's Dale and Ike?"

"Been out most o' the day," replied Sody. "Left after we got back from town. Dale wanted to check on some cattle over in the south range. They'll be back in time for supper."

"What am I going to do?" Peter asked anxiously.

"There isn't much you can do," said Silent. "You might saddle up and see if you can find the masked man, but I wouldn't suggest it."

"That letter—it means so much," said Peter.

"To you—and to someone else," grunted Silent. "Well, as long as the boys are out, we'll head back to town."

"Won't ya stay for supper?" asked Sody.

"Not this time, Sody," replied Silent as they walked over to their horses. "We'll take you up on that another time. I'd like to see Dale and talk with him."

"I'll tell him," said Peter. "But what will I say to that lawyer?"

"Just sit tight," advised Silent. "I'll tell him what happened—just in case he doesn't already know about the suitcase. See you soon."

Irish and Silent mounted and rode back toward town. But as they neared Flat Bottom, Silent suggested that they ride around town and head for the mesa. Irish grinned. He knew that his partner's curiosity was getting the best of him.

When they swung up on the mesa, Silent slowed his horse down to a walk, and studied the road carefully. At last he found the place where the stage had stopped today. He could see that the wheels on the right side had gone off the road slightly, digging into the loose dirt.

"Here's where the stage was stopped a short time back," he said, straightening in his saddle and pointing to the wheel marks.

"Good. Now what?" asked Irish, looking around.

"Let's search the surrounding area," suggested Silent. "You take the right side and I'll take the left. Crisscross and see if you find anything. That fellow wouldn't want to cart that suitcase very far just in case he bumped into someone. Probably opened it, got that letter, and dumped the case."

They rode off, crisscrossing the area. Swinging in and out of the brush was a slow procedure, but neither man was to be deterred.

Irish was the one who spotted the suitcase. It was closed, but the two straps around it had been cut with a knife.

Silent said, "Well, we might as well ride back to town and see that lawyer. We won't say we found the suit-case. Then after supper we'll ride out to the Box B. Let Peter open the suitcase. But I bet he won't find that letter."

Clay Bannister looked up at the two cowboys as they entered his small law office.

"I heard that a masked man held up the stage and stole the suitcase," he said sarcastically. "I suppose he has that letter."

"We wouldn't know," said Silent. "But why did he just take the suitcase?"

"Suppose you ask him," snapped Bannister.

"I reckon I will," said Silent and stamped out of the office, with Irish following him.

Bannister glared at their backs and shook his head, then picked up a telegram from the top of his desk. It said:

WILL LEAVE TODAY. ARRIVE FRIDAY. ANNIE BENSON.

The lawyer chuckled as he put the telegram in a desk drawer.

After supper, Silent Slade and Irish O'Day headed for the Box B ranch. It was about dark when they arrived. The hired men and Peter were just finishing their supper and Sody invited the visitors to join them in a piece of apple pie. Irish sat down in the kitchen, but Silent refused.

He handed the suitcase to Peter. "We found it near where the latest holdup took place."

Peter looked at it, then at Silent. "Someone cut the straps." He put it down on a chair and opened it. "Looks like someone went through everything."

"Is that letter there?" asked Silent.

Peter rummaged through things very carefully, then straightened, shaking his head.

"It's gone!"

"You mean someone stopped the stage just to get that letter?" asked Dale Boyd as he pushed back from the table and walked over to Peter.

"That's about the size of it," replied Silent. "To prevent you from claiming this ranch. That letter could possibly interfere with some well-laid plans."

"How'd the holdup man know that letter was in my suitcase?" asked Peter.

"When you told that lawyer, I suppose word spread," said Silent. "Anyway, it's gone."

"Do you think we can find it?" asked Peter.

Silent shook his head. "I doubt it," he replied. "I suppose the man who got it read it, then burned it. I know that's what I would have done."

"So Peter's chances of gettin' this ranch aren't too good, are they?" grunted Sody.

"Right now, his chances are pretty slim," said Silent.

"Who'll get it?" asked Sody.

"I understand there's supposed to be a niece, Annie Benson, who'll claim the Box B," replied Silent.

"Ol' Jim never mentioned anyone except Pete," said Sody. "Huh! A woman runnin' this spread! No, sir!" He shook his head violently. "If that comes to be, I'm pullin' out. Never did think this was a permanent position."

"How long you been here, Sody?" asked Irish.

"Well, when Bubblin' River was a stream an' those hills just mounds o' dirt," replied Sody. "I came here with ol' Jim 'bout forty years ago."

"Supposin' everyone waits to see what will happen," suggested Dale. "We all love this place. And if we have to, we'll fight for it."

"Let's hope we don't have to fight," said Peter.

"Let's hope not," sighed Silent. "Dale, could I have a word with you?"

"Sure," said the foreman.

They walked out to the front porch and sat down.

"What's on your mind, Silent?"

"Why did Jim Benson write the cattlemen's association for help?" asked Silent.

"He claimed that we're losin' cows," Dale replied. "But we never had any proof of it. Jim was bad at takin' counts. It's been at least five years since the last count."

"Why didn't he take a count each year?"

"Thought it was a waste of time," replied Dale. "Besides, Jim was too busy with other things besides runnin' the Box B. I think that's why he wanted Peter to come here an' take over the ranch for him."

"I heard Jim was a partner in the Golden Eagle."

Dale nodded. "Yes, that was prob'ly his biggest investment. But he also owned interest in the hotel, the bank, and the Silver Coin Saloon. I dunno how much, but I reckon it was plenty."

"Why was Jim shot?"

Dale shook his head and sighed. "I haven't the slightest idea, Silent," he replied. "He was so well liked around here. He left the ranch, headin' for town to pick up the mail. And about three hours later, me an' Ike started for town and we found him. We took him to the doctor's house, but he never regained consciousness, so it's all a puzzle to us. Ike, Sody, an' me have gone over it time and again tryin' to find an answer."

"Did Jim always go in for the mail?"

"Yes," nodded Dale. "You could set your watch by him. For years he rode in every mornin'. Usually checked on things he was interested in, had a drink or two, an' rode back."

"What do you think about Peter?"

"Nice young fellow," replied the foreman. "Old Jim spoke a lot about him in the past few months and prayed that he'd come here and learn ranchin' so he could take over this place an' Jim could relax with his other interests."

"Never heard him mention an Annie Benson?"

Dale shook his head. "Never a word," he replied. "It seems too crazy to talk about. Jim never, in the fifteen years I've been with him, mentioned any relative but his brother, Earl, in San Francisco, and his nephew, Peter. When Earl died, Peter wrote Jim about it. He took it hard, although he hadn't seen Earl in many years. But they did write. I hear Earl left a bundle to Peter."

"Well, we'll have to see what happens when Annie Benson gets here," said Silent. "It might be most interesting. Maybe you can look through some old letters Jim received from his brother or Peter and keep them around in case we might need them."

"We?" queried Dale. "What's your interest, Silent?"

"Jim asked for help, so we have an interest."

CHAPTER FOUR

The stage from Custer reached Flat Bottom on time Friday afternoon. Clay Bannister was waiting for it at the livery stable.

A short distance away, half hidden in the shadows of a doorway, stood Silent Slade watching the arrival. He soon saw a young lady step down from the stage, with Bannister assisting her.

"Annie Benson," Silent muttered, an amused expression on his lean face. "I'm glad she got here safely." He rushed off to the hotel.

Bannister greeted the young lady and forgot to let go of her hand until she pulled it free.

"Sorry," he muttered. "It isn't often I have the pleasure of welcoming such a charming person to Flat Bottom."

"Oh, thank you," smiled the young lady, who looked to be about twenty-two. She had an oval face, with silky auburn hair and big blue eyes, and a very fetching figure.

"Is this Flat Bottom?" she asked.

"Indeed it is," replied Bannister, pointing toward the right. "Our main street is over there."

Buster came around the stage, struggling with three suitcases, which he dumped at her feet.

"Your luggage, ma'am," he said, then turned and entered the office.

"I'll take them," said Bannister. "I believe you'll stay at the hotel until we have everything settled."

"I thought I was to own a big ranch," she said.

"There are legal formalities," said Bannister. "But there really is nothing to worry about. I hope to have it cleared up by Monday."

"You—you mean I have to live in a hotel until Monday?"

"Yes," nodded Bannister. "But you should be used to it. I understand you lived in a hotel in Phoenix."

Annie Benson shrugged her shoulders disgustedly and picked up one of the suitcases. Bannister picked up the other two, and they headed for the main street.

"That's the new owner of the Box B?" Emory Hill asked the stage driver.

"Uh-huh," nodded Buster. "I'll betcha she let me

know that ten times before we left Custer. I feel bad for the boys out there."

Silent and Irish were sitting on the hotel porch when Annie and Bannister came walking over. Both men smiled as the pair entered the establishment.

"Man, she's a beauty," muttered Irish.

"Shove your eyeballs back in," said Silent. "I don't think she'll ever give a cowboy a second look."

"Now that the parade is past, what are we goin' to do?" asked Irish.

"Wait a while, then check the register and see what she put down. I'm curious about her."

"Hold on. I spoke first," said Irish.

"Our minds are far apart, cowboy," said Silent. "Hey, here come the boys from the Box B."

"Looks like one o' those rides leading up to a battle," said Irish as he pointed in the opposite direction where four other riders were moving toward the Box B riders.

Dale led his group to the hitchrack in front of the hotel, while the other group pulled up in front of the Silver Coin Saloon. The riders at the saloon waved and called to the Box B group before going through the batwing doors. One of them turned and walked across the street.

Peter, Dale, Ike, and Sody came up to where Silent and Irish were sitting. But they turned as the person coming across the street approached them.

"Howdy, Debby," greeted Dale.

Silent and Irish jerked around in their chairs to look at

Debby. She took off her hat and shook her head, letting waves of brown hair fall to her shoulders. She was a very attractive young lady with flashing brown eyes and a big smile.

"Hey, I wanted you to meet some folks new to Flat Bottom," said Dale. Then he introduced Peter, Silent, and Irish. "Miss Nelson is the daughter of Mike Nelson, who owns the Lazy N ranch."

They all shook hands and Debby looked curiously at Peter.

"Are you going to run the Box B?" she asked.

"I'm not sure," replied Peter. "There seem to be some complications."

"I'm sorry to hear about your uncle. He was a good friend of our family, and we'll all miss him," she said softly.

"I only wish I could have known him," said Peter.

"What you doin' in town, Debby?" asked Dale.

"Just needed a change, Dale," she replied, "and the boys all wanted to quench their thirst. So we decided to come in here and have supper. I don't know if the boys will remember or not after a few drinks."

"We'll see that you're in good company," said Peter. "We plan to stay here for the evening."

"It might interest you to know that Annie Benson showed up on the stage today," said Silent.

"She did, huh?" grunted Peter, shaking his head. "I don't know what to do about her."

"Wait'll you see her," said Irish. "She's a city beauty —lost out here in a cow town."

"I suppose I should meet her—if she's my cousin," said Peter.

"I thought you were Jim Benson's only living relative," said Debby.

"That's what I thought, too, but that lawyer says Uncle Jim's will gives everything to Annie Benson. I never heard of her."

Debby looked around at the six men, shaking her head.

"He never mentioned any niece, only a nephew in San Francisco."

"Let's just wait and see what happens," suggested Silent. "They can't do a thing until Monday now."

"When do you want to eat?" Peter asked Debby, and the others grinned.

"Oh, after a while. I want to go into a few stores first."

"Fine, I'll go with you," said Peter. "I haven't seen any of the stores in Flat Bottom."

He took her by the arm and they went into a small shop just beyond the sheriff's office.

"He's a fast worker," said Irish.

"I hope he's that fast when he faces that lawyer," said Dale. "C'mon, let's join the Lazy N group."

Silent and Irish declined, but the others followed Dale across the street and into the Silver Coin Saloon.

"Peter and Debby make a nice couple," said Irish.

"Think you're Cupid, eh?" said Silent as he got up from his chair and stretched. "That lawyer's sure spending a lot of time with Annie."

Irish followed Silent into the lobby. They went up to the desk and looked at the register. Just below Peter's name was: Annie Benson, Phoenix, Arizona.

"Writes a nice hand," remarked Irish.

"Uh-huh," nodded Silent.

Just then someone stepped into the lobby. Silent turned to see Neal Thompson of the Golden Eagle Mine.

Thompson glanced around, then came up to the counter and rang for the clerk, who appeared through a doorway in back of the counter.

"Hello, Mr. Thompson," said the clerk. "What can I do for you?"

"I understand Clay Bannister is here. I must see him," replied Thompson.

"Yes, he brought in a young lady who, I understand, will take over the Box B ranch," said the clerk. "They're in room 7 upstairs."

Thompson nodded and hurried up the stairs. The clerk looked at Silent and Irish.

"Anythin' I can do for you?"

"No," replied Silent. "We were just curious as to who the young lady was that was with Bannister."

"She just came in on the stage," said the clerk. "My, what confusion there is over the Box B ranch. First Peter Benson, now this lady. I wonder who'll get the ranch."

"I hope the one who deserves it," replied Silent. He and Irish decided to visit the sheriff then.

Wilbur Wendell and Harry Baylor were in the office, the sheriff at his desk going through mail that had come in on the stage, while Harry sat on a cot against the wall, cleaning his six-shooter. They looked up as Silent and Irish entered.

"Well, what's the good word today?" asked the sheriff.

"Annie Benson's arrived," said Silent.

"Has, huh? I saw Peter Benson an' Debby Nelson walkin' past here a while ago," said the sheriff. "This could be somethin' very interestin'."

"I'm sure it will be," said Silent. "What do you know about Thompson of the Golden Eagle?"

"Oh, Neal Thompson's a great fellow," said Wilbur. "Right now he's in a bind tryin' to figure out who's who in regard to the operation of the mine. With Charley King, Fred Hansen, an' Jim Benson dead, it leaves him as sole survivor. He made arrangements for shipping King and Hansen back East to the relatives, but he hasn't heard from them regarding their takin' over the shares each man had in the mine. As for Benson, that's goin' to have to wait at least until after Monday when the judge will hear the readin' of the will."

"I can see Thompson has a problem," said Silent. "Is Bannister the attorney for the mine?"

"I believe he is," said Wilbur. "Bein' the only lawyer hereabouts, he gets most of the work."

Just then a sound at the door caused the four men to look in that direction. There stood Peter Benson, bedecked in a Western outfit. He looked so different that it was a moment before the men recognized him. He wore a light-blue shirt, Levi's, fancy high-heeled boots, and on his head was a tan-colored Stetson. Around his waist was a gun belt, and on his right hip was a holster with a gun.

"Gone Western!" snorted Irish.

"How do you like it?" asked the young man, coming into the office and urging Debby Nelson to follow him. "Debby helped me choose the clothes."

"Looks like a real cowboy," said Silent. "Don't think I'd have recognized you, Peter."

"Debby, you done made a true Westerner out of Pete," said Harry.

"He might as well dress the part," laughed Debby. "It was nice to go shopping with a man who didn't mind spending some money."

"What's money for but to spend?" said Peter. Then he turned to Debby. "C'mon, let's get supper."

They walked out of the office, and the four men laughed.

"What a pair they make," said Wilbur, shaking his head. "Hope that young one is careful with his money. He don't know what might happen here."

"He's not dependent on taking over that ranch," said Silent. "I hear he has a nice bank account left to him by his father."

"Some people have all the luck," growled Harry.

"You have luck," said a voice from the rear of the building. "Lettin' me sit here an' waste away."

Harry turned and looked toward the jail cells at the rear, then at Wilbur Wendell, who was also puzzled.

"When did you put someone in there?" demanded Wilbur.

"I—I—" stammered Harry. "I never put no one in there."

"Well, somebody with a badge put me in here," snapped the voice.

Irish glanced at Silent, who was pretending to be looking at a reward notice tacked on the wall. Irish knew of his partner's ability to throw his voice, and he was always amused at what happened.

Harry put his six-shooter down on the cot, got to his feet, and walked to the back, peering into the three cells. But they were empty. He turned and looked at the sheriff.

"No one's here. But, Wilbur, you heard that voice, didn't you?"

"I sure did," said the sheriff. He, too, walked over to the three cells, scratching his head, looking puzzled. Then he looked at Silent and Irish.

"Did you boys hear a voice back here?" he asked.

"We heard a voice," replied Irish. "No one there, eh?"

The two law officers came back and sat down where they had been before. Harry picked up his six-shooter, and the voice was heard again.

"You don't need that gun to shoot me—just starve me to death here in this cell."

The two lawmen looked at each other, then back at the cells.

"What in hell's goin' on?" demanded the sheriff. "Them cells are empty."

Irish looked at Silent as Silent turned away from the reward poster and came back to his chair. The two law officers looked at Silent and Irish.

"Are we crazy?" asked Harry.

"No, I don't think so," replied Silent, a smile on his lean face. "Sure no one is back there?"

"Positive of it," snapped the sheriff.

"Then it must have come in through one of the windows," suggested Silent.

"What?" said Harry, glancing back to the cells. Each had a small window at the rear, near the ceiling. "No one could look in any of those windows an' see me with this gun."

Irish started to laugh, and they all looked at him. He shook his head, took a deep breath, and pointed at Silent.

"Sorry, Silent, but I've got to tell them," he said. "It was Silent."

"Huh?" gasped the sheriff. "How could it have been him? He was standing over by the wall reading a notice."

"It's very simple," explained Silent. "Have you ever heard about ventriloquism?"

"What's that—a religion?" asked Harry.

"No, dummy!" said the sheriff. "It means a person can throw his voice." He squinted thoughtfully at Silent. "Did you do that?"

Silent nodded, and he gave them a demonstration. The two lawmen sat there amazed.

"I used to do it on the stage," said Silent, getting to his feet. "We better leave you gents to your newfound friend in the cell. It's time to eat."

"Thanks, Silent," said the voice in the cell.

Both officers turned and glanced at the cells, then turned back, shaking their heads as Silent and Irish walked out of the office.

"Can you beat that?" said Harry. "I wish I could do that."

"An' prob'ly get shot for doin' it," grunted Wilbur.

In the cafe Silent and Irish found Debby and Peter at a back table, eating and talking earnestly to each other. As Silent and Irish sat down, Thompson, Annie, and Bannister entered the place. They took a table by the front window. The lawyer looked back at Peter and smiled, but he did not say anything.

Before Silent and Irish had finished eating, the men from both the Box B and the Lazy N sauntered in and sat at the counter. Then one of them, an elderly man, got up and walked over to where Debby was eating. She quickly introduced him to Peter as her father, Mike Nelson. The owner of the Lazy N pulled up a chair and sat down.

"So you're the one that's goin' to take over the Box B, eh?" he asked.

"I'm not sure of that," replied Peter. "I believe I have some competition from that little lady at the front table with the lawyer and the other man."

Nelson half turned and looked at Annie. Then he turned back to Peter.

"What's she got to do with it?"

"My uncle's will seems to have left everything to her," said Peter.

"Nonsense!" said the rancher. "I heard Jim speak about you but never about any other relative."

"My proof of everything was stolen yesterday when a masked man held up the stage and took my suitcase, opened it, and took out the letter. Then he hid the suitcase, but those two gents over there, Slade and O'Day, found it and brought it to me, minus my letter from Uncle Jim telling me I was his only living relative."

"That sure makes it bad," said Mike Nelson. "What are you goin' to do?"

"Right now sit tight," replied Peter.

"What else can he do, Daddy?" asked Debby.

"I couldn't answer that," Nelson said, getting to his feet. "We'll pick you up in the hotel lobby when we finish," he told Debby and went back to his counter seat.

When Silent and Irish finished, Silent handed some money to Irish to pay the bill. Then he walked over to the front table where Annie, Bannister, and Thompson were seated.

"Just wanted to find out when you were going to read the will," Silent said, looking at Bannister.

"What business is it of yours?" snorted the lawyer.

"I'm checking for Peter Benson," replied Silent.

Bannister laughed and shook his head.

"He hasn't got a chance, Slade. Why doesn't he go back to Frisco?"

"Because he's here to claim his uncle's ranch." Silent looked at Annie and smiled. "You have a nice wardrobe, Miss Benson. Suppose you purchased most of it at the shops on Cannel Avenue in Phoenix. I visited them once or twice."

She smiled. "Yes, I always buy my clothes there."

Silent smiled back and walked out of the cafe to find Irish waiting for him. Then Debby and Peter came out and headed for the hotel lobby.

"Trying to get in good with the lawyer—or the young lady?" queried Irish.

"Both," replied Silent. "Part of the puzzle is falling into place, but there are still some missing parts."

"I'm glad to see you're happy," said Irish. "How much longer are we goin' to stay here?"

"That all depends," replied Silent.

"Yeah? On what?"

"On those missing parts, Irish. I've got to find them."

"And when you do, then we can move on, huh?" asked Irish.

The cowboys from the Lazy N, led by Mike Nelson, came out of the cafe and passed Silent and Irish as they went into the hotel lobby where Debby and Peter had gone. After a few minutes, they all came out on the walk. Peter stayed there while the others crossed the street to their horses and headed out of town. Peter waved to them, then saw Silent and Irish and moved over to the pair.

"Seems to me like you've found something mighty interesting," remarked Irish as he looked at Peter.

"She's great," said Peter. "She spent some time in San Francisco and she knew places I knew, so we had a lot to talk about."

"That made it nice," said Silent, looking at the young man. "Know how to use that new gun?"

"A little," replied Peter. "I wanted to be a policeman, so I studied law and learned the use of firearms. I used to go to the police target range once a week and practice."

"That's good," nodded Silent. "But out here it's life and death. There's no chance to practice, and you don't want to miss. Maybe you won't get a second time."

"That's what Sody told me," said Peter. "He's going to show me how to fast draw."

"Do it with an empty gun," warned Irish. "I've seen too many people lose toes practicing with a loaded gun."

The Box B boys came out of the cafe then.

"Let's get back to the ranch!" Dale called to Peter.

Peter nodded to Silent and Irish and followed the others to the hotel hitchrack where their horses were tied.

"That young fellow—if he lives—might amount to somethin'," observed Irish.

"There's a good chance," said Silent. "Let's go over to the saloon and see the place. We've been here a few days and never visited that den."

The saloon was nearly empty at this time of evening. A couple of men were at the bar drinking beer and talking. The bartender was cleaning the large mirror in back of the bar, and two men were playing cards at one of the tables.

Silent and Irish walked up to the bar and ordered drinks. A moment later Clay Bannister and Neal

Thompson came into the saloon and joined the two men who were drinking beer.

"Lawyer without his little charge," Irish softly said to Silent.

Silent toyed with his glass and looked at the four men down the bar from them. "He and Thompson seem pretty thick," he said softly.

The bartender walked over to them and asked if they were ready for another drink.

"Thanks, but one's the limit," said Silent. "Who are those two men that Bannister and Thompson are talking to?"

The bartender replied, "That's Clyde Duggan, an' the younger one's his son, Chuck. They own the Double D ranch south of town."

"Thanks," said Silent.

He put his glass down on the bar and walked over to an empty card table. Sitting down, he picked up the deck of cards that lay on the table and began manipulating them in various designs. Irish moved over, watching him, and the bartender also came over.

"This table isn't—" He stopped, his eyes wide as he watched Silent. "I—shucks! I never seen anythin' like that."

"He's just foolin' around," said Irish. "You should see him when he's warmed up."

Silent spread out the deck, face down across the table, and looked up at the bartender.

"Take a card and don't let me see it," said Silent.

The bartender carefully pulled out a card and held it up close to his face.

Silent stacked the other cards and held them out to the bartender.

"Take this deck, turn your back, and put your card into the deck anywhere you want. Then put the deck back down on the table."

The bartender did as instructed.

"Your card's in the deck?" queried Silent.

"It sure is," nodded the bartender. "Now what?"

Silent smiled as he picked up the deck and began to fan through it. Suddenly a card shot out and flew to the floor.

"Pick it up," said Silent to the bartender.

The bartender did so and handed it to Silent, who looked at it.

"Why, that's the card next in number to the one you took before," said Silent.

The bartender looked amazed.

Silent shook his head and put the deck back on the table, glancing up at the bartender. "I thought you said you put your card back into the deck."

"I did," the bartender snapped. "I put it in with the other cards."

Silent pushed his chair back, got to his feet, and moved close to the bartender, looking curiously at him.

"What's the matter?" asked the bartender.

Silent pulled a card out of the man's shirt pocket. "You lied to me." He showed the card to the bartender.

"I—I never—never—I put it in the deck," the bartender stammered.

"Are you sure you did?" asked Silent.

"Yeah—yeah, I did. I swear I did!"

"All right, then you did," laughed Silent. "That is the card, isn't it?"

"It is, but how did it get in my pocket?" asked the bewildered man.

"Must have jumped in there," replied Silent. "Thanks for the use of your cards."

The bartender stood there holding the card, shaking his head, as Silent and Irish walked out of the saloon.

"Hey, Ben, get over here and take care of us!" called Thompson.

The bartender walked over to the four men, still dazed at what he had witnessed.

"Ben, what's the matter?" asked Bannister.

"That tall cowpoke," he said. "He—he—aw, you'd never believe what he did with the cards. What's your order, gents?"

CHAPTER FIVE

Peter Benson, in his new Levi's, walked out to the corral where Dale Boyd and Ike Jones were checking their horses.

"Want to ride?" Dale asked Peter.

"Yes, I was thinking of taking a ride," replied Peter. "But I'd like a tame horse."

"Get you one," Dale said. "Goin' to town?"

"Well, I don't think so," replied Peter. "I was thinking of riding over to the Lazy N."

Dale laughed and selected a horse. Ike helped him saddle the horse and brought it out to Peter.

"The Lazy N is south of here, isn't it?" asked Peter.

Dale nodded. "Your best bet is to follow the river

south until you come to the first road and bridge. Turn west and you're almost in the ranch yard."

Peter mounted. "I'll be back this afternoon," he told them, then rode away.

"Love bug's got him," laughed Ike.

"I believe it has," nodded Dale. "Hope he don't get lost."

"He can't if he follows the river."

Peter rode south, passing the town of Flat Bottom. A little farther on, the trees along the river became more dense, slowing him down. Suddenly his horse halted, holding up its head.

"What's the matter?" asked Peter.

Wham! A bullet whistled past his head, and he dropped the reins. When a second shot rang out, Peter fell out of the saddle, sprawling on the ground.

Debby Nelson and her father were riding across the bridge on their way to Flat Bottom when they heard the two shots. They drew rein, looking around.

"It sounded from down along the east side of the river," said the old rancher and looked in that direction.

"Perhaps someone hunting," said Debby.

"Could be, but at this time of year what's there to hunt?" snorted the old man. "Let's just look things over."

Debby saw a lone rider galloping away from the trees and across the barren land.

"Look, Daddy—that rider's in an awful hurry!"

"We'll check along the river an' see if he left someone behind."

They did so.

"Daddy, there's someone on the ground!"

Mike Nelson and Debby both dismounted quickly and came over to Peter, who looked up at them, blood smeared across his face.

"What happened to you, Peter?" Debby asked, kneeling beside him.

"I don't know," he replied weakly. "Someone shot at me. Missed the first shot, but I guess he hit me the second time."

Mike Nelson knelt on the other side of Peter and quickly made an examination.

"Crease along the side of his head," he announced. "Debby, get some water from the river."

Debby bounced to her feet and went to the river. She took off her hat and half filled it with water, then returned. The old man had taken out a red bandana from his hip pocket. Now he quickly dipped it into the water and began to wash Peter's face.

"Boy, that feels good," said Peter.

"Did you see who shot you?" asked the old man.

"I never saw a soul," replied Peter. "My horse stopped and seemed to be distracted by something. Then I was shot at."

Debby produced a very large handkerchief, which she tied around his head.

"Thank you—both of you," Peter said.

"We're takin' you in to Doc's house," said Mike.

"Neither of us are much at doctorin', so it's better to have a professional check it."

"I don't want to put you folks out," said Peter as he started to get to his feet.

But his knees were weak, so Mike and Debby helped him.

"We were going into town," said Debby. "Lucky we heard those shots."

"It certainly was," replied Peter, then looked around. "Where's my horse?"

"Prob'ly took off at the shootin'," said Mike. "My bronc rides double."

"So does mine, Daddy," said Debby.

The old man looked at his daughter, then turned to Peter.

"Reckon I'm overruled, young fellow."

Debby had Peter get in the saddle. Then she climbed on behind him.

When Peter and the Nelsons arrived at Doc Schulte's house, they found the sheriff and Silent Slade with the doctor. The three men looked curiously at Peter as he came into the front room, followed by Debby and Mike.

"What's this all about?" demanded the sheriff.

"A man shot Peter," Debby replied quickly. "We found him. Daddy cleaned the wound, but he needs a doctor to check it."

Doc Schulte led Peter over to a chair next to the window and he carefully removed the white handkerchief and looked at the wound. The sheriff and Silent moved closer and looked at it also.

"Where did it happen?" asked the sheriff.

"Along the river between the Box B and the Lazy N," replied Mike. "He was comin' over to visit us."

Doc winked at Peter. "Well, you'll live, so don't worry. Come with me into the back room and I'll clean it some more and bandage it for you."

While Peter followed Doc into the back of the house, Mike and Debby left the place.

The sheriff looked at Silent.

"What next?" he muttered.

"This country isn't safe for anyone," said Silent. "Again it was one man."

"Yeah, but which man?" growled Wilbur. "There's too many men in this valley to pick out just one. Why shoot at the kid?"

"Why did they steal that letter from him?" said Silent.

"To keep him from gettin' the Box B," said Wilbur.

Silent nodded. "That's the only answer to that question. But who? Who's really behind it?"

"And the Box B is a good outfit," said the sheriff. "But not worth killin' over. Not if you ask me."

"I have to disagree with you," said Silent. "Why did they kill Jim Benson? Why try to kill Peter?"

Wilbur Wendell shook his head.

"It just don't make sense, that's all. Why, this is the second attempt on Peter's life."

"I hope there's not a third time," grunted Silent as Peter returned with his head bandaged, followed by Doc and Mrs. Schulte.

"He's going to be fine," announced Doc.

Peter looked around. "Where's Debby?"

"She and her father went on their errands, I guess," replied the sheriff.

"Did, huh?" Peter picked up his hat, which he had carried into town, and went out the front door in quest of Debby.

Doc said, "Now, gentlemen, as I told you just before they came in, I took out the bullets from Jim Benson, Charley King and Fred Hansen. Would you care to see them?"

"I would," nodded Silent.

"What good will old bullets do?" queried the sheriff as Doc crossed the room to a desk.

He pulled out the middle drawer and took out a cigar box, which he opened. Inside were several bullets, each with a little tag wired onto it.

"I've kept all the bullets that have killed people since I came here ten years ago," Doc said as he fingered through them, selecting three and placing them on the desk top.

Silent picked them up and read the tag on each one. Then he carried them over to the window where he had better light to study them by.

"Blasted fool!" muttered the sheriff. "A bullet's a bullet."

Silent ignored the sheriff's remark. He carefully looked at each one, turning it over with his fingers. Finally he placed all three in the palm of his hand. With one finger he gently moved them around a little. A smile crossed his face as he closed his hand on the bullets and came back to the desk. There he placed them in the cigar box.

"Well?" queried the sheriff, peering closely at Silent.

"Bullets tell you things," said Silent.

"I never heard nothin'," snorted Wilbur.

"Years ago an old range detective explained to me about bullets," said Silent. "His name was Goober Glendon. He used bullets to clear up many cases that he was working on."

"Huh!" grunted Wilbur. "Lemme see those bullets."

Silent winked at Doc as he turned and walked out of the house, leaving a puzzled law officer looking at the bullets in the cigar box.

Irish and Harry Baylor were in the Silver Coin Saloon testing their ability at pool when Silent slipped into the place. He walked over to them.

"It's a toss-up between us," said Irish. "What did you and the sheriff find out?"

"I found out some interesting things," said Silent.

"What about Wilbur?" Harry asked after he took his shot—and missed.

"He'll be along presently," replied Silent. "I left him looking at a box full of bullets."

Harry shook his head and looked at Irish.

"I've had enough. What about you?"

"Me, too," nodded Irish.

"I'll buy a drink," offered the deputy as they placed their cues on the table.

"Not now," said Irish, glancing at Silent. He figured his friend had something on his mind. "I'll see you later, Harry."

Silent walked outside, followed by Irish. They

crossed the street and sat down on the hotel porch.

"For Saturday afternoon, there's not too much activity in town," observed Silent.

"You didn't come over here just to tell me that," said Irish.

"No, that's true," Silent said. "Those bullets, the ones from Benson, King, and Hansen all match. Fired from the same gun."

"Huh!" said Irish. "Does the sheriff know that?"

"Not yet," said Silent. "I left him looking at them. I don't suppose he saw anything unusual. They're all .45's, and there must be a burr in the barrel that caused each of them to have a scratch the length of the bullet. None of the other bullets in the box had that scratch."

"Can you beat that?" said Irish. "All from the—"

Irish halted in mid-sentence as he saw Dale Boyd, Ike Jones, and Sody Smith come riding down the main street leading Peter's horse. They swung in at the hitchrack in front of the hotel and looked at Silent and Irish.

"We're missin' a young one," said Dale.

"He's around here somewhere," said Silent. "Last time I saw him, he left the doctor's house in quest of a fair maiden."

"Thank goodness!" said Sody. "We could imagine all kinds of things when his horse came back alone."

"He was shot," said Silent, "but not bad. A crease on the left side of his head. Didn't stop him in his quest."

"How'd he get into town?" asked Dale.

"Debby and her father found him. They heard the shots and investigated and found him," replied Silent.

"Just look around, and you'll find him."

"That's love for you!" grunted Sody. "He's just run-nin' around while we worry ourselves sick."

The sheriff came around the corner and headed for the group.

"All right, smart cowboy, them bullets are all the same," he snapped at Silent. "Think you're smart, eh? Well, me an' Doc checked 'em. They're all alike."

"What's this all about?" asked Dale.

"Bullets—you know, them pieces of lead that kill people," said Wilbur Wendell.

"Well, what about bullets?" asked Dale.

"They tell tales," said Silent. "But you can't hear them, only see them."

"I think you're crazy, Slade," snorted the sheriff. "No dumb cowpoke can kid with me."

"Sheriff," said Dale quickly, "Slade's an assoc—" He stopped short as he realized what he was about to say.

"He's a what?" demanded the sheriff. "Go ahead, finish it."

Dale looked helplessly at Silent, who sighed deeply.

"This can't go any further than right here, among this little group," said Silent. "It's dangerous."

"What's all this hocus-pocus about?" asked the sher-iff.

"Slade is an association detective," said Dale softly.

The sheriff looked quickly from Dale to Silent.

"Jim Benson asked for help," said Silent. "We got here too late."

"I can't believe it," muttered Wilbur, rubbing the back of his neck.

"You heard it. Now don't repeat it," cautioned Irish. "Knowledge of it could mean our death."

"And for your information, Sheriff," said Silent, "the bullets that killed Benson, King, and Hansen were fired from the same gun."

"That's what you found out at Doc's, eh?" Wilbur said.

"Yes," nodded Silent. "I'll show you later how I found out."

Just then Peter and Debby left the cafe and walked to the hotel.

Dale stepped toward Peter. "It's good to see you. We were worried when your bronc came home alone."

Peter looked at the horse standing at the hitchrack.

"Glad you brought it in," he said.

"Peter's fine now," announced Debby as her father came out of the cafe and joined them. "But watch him. Someone doesn't want him around."

"Perhaps you should leave here," suggested the sheriff.

"Oh, no, I'm staying here," said Peter as he looked at Debby. "I've found what I've been searching for for years. I've done nothing wrong, so why should anyone want to kill me? If the ranch really belongs to my cousin, she can have it. But I'm sure the truth will be found out whether I'm dead or alive."

CHAPTER SIX

The Silver Coin Saloon was pretty quiet when Silent Slade and Irish O'Day stopped in for a drink.

"How much longer are we going to stay in this burg?" queried Irish as they sat down at a table with their filled glasses.

"I'm not sure," replied Silent, looking at his drink. "I have a feeling that things will come to a head Monday when that will is read."

"We'll wait till then, huh?"

Silent nodded as he slowly sipped his drink. Just then Clay Bannister entered the saloon. He walked directly to the bar and ordered a whiskey. Then he spoke with two or three of the other customers.

"Prominent man," said Irish softly. "I'd hate to be loved like he is."

Silent nodded. "Prominence isn't everything, cowboy. Those that get too high sure have a long way to fall. Well, I thought the Box B crowd might come in to let Peter have a sample of his first Saturday night in Arizona," said Silent. "Maybe he's had enough excitement for one day, though."

Chuck Duggan stepped into the room right then. He sauntered up to the bar, stopping next to Bannister, who turned from the men he was talking with and spoke to Duggan. Duggan said something to the lawyer. And soon they edged their way down the bar away from the other men.

Silent watched them as he finished his drink. They seemed to be in very earnest conversation. Then Bannister bought Duggan a drink. When Duggan finished, they left the saloon.

Silent got to his feet and walked to the doorway. He paused there and looked out at the dark street. There was enough lantern light for him to see the two men stop by the hitchrack for a moment. Duggan untied the reins of his horse, and then they walked up the street and around the corner.

Silent motioned for Irish to remain in the saloon. Then he stepped out and followed them, pausing at the corner of the hotel. He could see Duggan with his horse standing in front of the livery stable. After several minutes, Bannister came out leading a saddled horse. They mounted and rode back to the main street.

Quickly Silent faded into the shadows of a doorway

and watched as they rode past and headed out of town. He smiled to himself. He had heard comments that Bannister visited the Double D ranch for a night or two now and then.

After a few minutes, Silent crossed the street and looked into the Silver Coin. He saw that Irish had company at the pool table in the person of Harry Baylor. So he moved down the street, pausing in front of Bannister's office. The door was locked and there were heavy drapes across the front window. Silent then walked around to the rear of Bannister's office. There was no window, just a solid door. Silent struck a match and examined the door. It looked as if it hadn't been used lately. The match almost burned his fingers before he dropped it and stepped on it. Then he took a key from his pocket—the hotel key—and tried it. It fit in the lock beneath the handle, but it wouldn't work. Not at first. Silent carefully moved it around, in and out. Suddenly it caught, and he was able to turn it. The door was unlocked.

Silent stepped inside, closing the door behind him. He paused, struck another match, and peered around. He was in a small back room with a bed and a dresser. Near the dresser there was another door, half open. Silent moved that way as his match burned out. He stepped into the main office and struck another match The heavy drapes would prevent anyone on the outside from seeing the light of the match.

Finding an oil lamp on the corner of the desk, Silent lighted it and put it on the floor. He sat down in Bannister's swivel chair and began going through his desk drawers. They revealed very little.

In the last drawer on the right side, however, Silent found some old correspondence, which he removed. He carefully examined each piece.

He found two letters from Jim Benson. They dealt with cattle shipments. One had a paragraph at the end that interested Silent:

Continue your correspondence with Bill Hansen. I believe he will come around to my offer. He would like to get even with his brother. I feel it is worth every dollar I placed upon it.

Silent folded the letter and put it in his hip pocket. What was so valuable? Was Bill Hansen related to Fred Hansen, the man who had been murdered? Silent decided to wait until later to look into that. Then he found another letter of interest:

Thank you, Clay, for two wonderful nights here. Yes, I am interested in what you told me. Just let me know and I can arrive there soon. Much love, Annie

Silent folded that letter and started to put it in his hip pocket, but then he changed his mind. He took the first letter out, and then he pulled off his right boot, took off his sock, and put both letters in his sock. Next he pulled the sock and boot on. He stood up and, after a few steps around, it felt all right. "Can't take a chance."

He moved over to the small safe in the corner. Getting down on his hands and knees, he looked at it. It was antiquated and Silent shook it. It nearly opened. He put his right ear against the tumbler as he carefully turned the handle. He heard it click. Then he turned the handle in the opposite direction until it clicked again and the door swung open.

Silent studied the safe. It contained very little. But right on top was an envelope marked "Jim Benson Will." He took the envelope out and looked at it. It wasn't sealed, so Silent opened it and took out a single page. He moved back to the swivel chair and sat down, holding the paper near the lamp. He read it carefully. He reread it, then folded the paper and again placed it in his sock.

After that he carefully closed the envelope and placed it in the safe. Then he closed the safe.

Silent blew out the lamp after placing it back on the desk, and carefully made his way to the rear door. When he stepped out into the dark alley, something struck him on the head. A second blow sent him staggering to the ground, unconscious.

A dark figure paused and looked at Silent, then moved into Bannister's office.

Irish and Harry Baylor sat down in chairs against the wall in the Silver Coin Saloon and rested. They had battled for over an hour at the pool table with neither one able to claim a clear-cut victory.

Dale Boyd came into the saloon and walked up to the bar where he had a drink. Then he saw the two sitting against the wall and came over to them.

"Where's Silent?" he asked.

"I don't know," replied Irish. "Maybe he went to bed. What brings you in at this time?"

"Things were dull at the ranch, so I thought I'd come in and see what was goin' on. But it looks kinda dull in here, too," replied Dale. "I asked Ike and Sody to come with me, but they refused. Peter was already in bed."

"I think it's about time I got to bed," grunted Irish, getting to his feet. "I'm worn as thin as a dime."

Just then the rear door of the saloon banged open, and an old-timer staggered toward the bar.

"There's a dead man out in the alley!" he blurted. "I seen him."

Everyone converged on the rear door, with Harry Baylor grabbing a lantern from a hook on the wall and Irish on his heels. They stepped into the dark alley and looked around.

"Over there," shouted the deputy, holding the lantern high. In the light, he could see a body sprawled in the middle of the alley.

They all hurried down there and turned the figure over.

Irish gasped, "It's Silent!"

He dropped to his knees beside his partner and felt his pulse.

"He's still alive. Let's get him to the doctor's," he told Harry.

Willing hands assisted in lifting Silent, and four men carried him to Doc Schulte's house. The doctor was just coming out, since someone had gone to fetch him. And right then Sheriff Wilbur Wendell joined the group.

Silent was carefully carried into a bedroom. Doc and Mrs. Schulte were there as he was placed on the bed. They quickly began examining him. After a few minutes, Doc looked at Irish, the sheriff, and the deputy.

"Lucky he's got a hard head," Doc said. "Seems he was struck twice by a blunt instrument—probably a gun barrel."

"He'll be all right then?" asked Irish anxiously.

Doc nodded. "He should be, but I don't know how long it will take. O'Day, supposing you assist me in undressing him and putting him in this bed."

The sheriff and deputy stepped out into the hallway, and Doc closed the door on them. He looked at Irish.

"How did it happen?" Doc asked.

"I wish I knew," replied Irish. He then told Doc that he had been in the Silver Coin Saloon with Harry Baylor when it happened.

They undressed Silent, pulling off his boots, but leaving his socks on. Doc called his wife, who returned with a bucket of hot water and towels. She quickly went to work cleaning up Silent's head. Then Doc examined the two bloody bumps carefully.

"I wonder if I should take a couple stitches," muttered Doc, looking at his wife.

"I don't think it's that bad," she said. "Good bandaging will pull the ends together, and they should heal with this salve I have."

Doc nodded and stepped next to Irish. They watched Mrs. Schulte quickly prepare the wounds. Then she bandaged them. When she stepped back, she looked proudly at her work.

Doc said, "Well, Irish, you better go get some rest and come back in the morning. He should be awake by then."

"I could stay here," said Irish.

"Out!" snapped Doc. "We can handle this all right."

Irish took one last looked at Silent, then left the room. He found the sheriff and deputy in the front room waiting for him.

"What was he doin' out there?" queried the sheriff.

"I dunno." Irish shook his head. "We'll have to wait until he wakes up to get an answer."

"We thought he went to the hotel," said Harry. "He musta been gone about an hour when ol' Barney came staggerin' in the saloon to make the announcement."

"What was Barney doin' out there?" growled the sheriff.

"Never took time to ask him," replied Harry. "Maybe I better go look for Barney."

"Good idea," grunted the sheriff, and Harry left the house.

"Hope he finds Barney," sighed Irish.

"If he does, Barney will prob'ly be so drunk that he won't know what he found or where by this time," grunted the sheriff.

"Where does Barney work?"

"Work?" chuckled Wilbur. "I don't think Barney ever worked. He just exists around town doin' odd jobs— enough for another drink."

Just then, as they started for the door, Harry Baylor came back with another man.

"Barney's dead!" the newcomer blurted.

The sheriff shook his head as he looked from his deputy to the other man.

"Well, what happened?" he asked.

The man said, "I had left the Silver Coin and was startin' for the livery stable when I heard a shot. It was on the side street, so I ran down there. But I didn't see anyone. I did hear a horse galloping away, though. Then I started to turn toward the stable, and I thought I saw somethin' on the walk. I moved in closer and there was Barney. I lighted a match. He was shot through the head."

Doc heard them and came out. They all hurried down the street to the place where several men were standing, one holding a lantern. Barney was draped over the edge of the boardwalk, half on, half off in the street. There was a pool of blood around him.

"Nothing I can do," sighed Doc. "Better bring him down to my place."

Someone located a blanket and they took the body away. Irish, the sheriff, and Harry walked to the corner by the hotel where they stopped.

"Nothin' we can do now," snorted the sheriff. "What a night!"

"Poor ol' Barney," sighed the deputy. "He never hurt a fly."

"Probably the one who busted Silent might have thought that Barney had seen the attack," suggested Irish.

"That's the opinion I got," grunted Wilbur. "Anyway,

that's what we'll be workin' on for the present."

"Perhaps Silent will be able to help us when he wakes up," said Harry.

"I certainly hope he will," nodded the sheriff. "Well, if nothing more happens tonight, we'll see you in the mornin', Irish."

Irish nodded as he went into the hotel. The clerk was leaning on the counter, smoking a cigar. He squinted at Irish through the cigar smoke.

"Too bad about Slade," he said.

"Uh-huh," nodded Irish. "Silent didn't come here earlier, did he?"

The clerk shook his head. "I seen him leave the saloon just after Clay Bannister and Chuck Duggan came out. He walked down the street toward the corner, and I didn't see him after that."

Irish went back outside and walked to the corner and looked around. He could see the lantern in front of the livery stable, so he walked over to the office there to find Buster Gavin and Emory Hill in a two-handed poker game. They looked up at Irish.

"We just heard what happened," said Emory. "Darn shame. How's your pardner goin' to be?"

"He'll pull through," said Irish. "Did either of you see him this evenin'?"

They glanced at each other, then shook their heads.

"Not much business. Clay Bannister got his horse and rode away with Chuck Duggan, but that's about all," replied Emory. "Heck of a Saturday night!"

Irish thanked them and went back to the Silver Coin Saloon. There were three men at a poker table and four at the bar, but that was all. He didn't recognize any of them. He walked up to the bar and the bartender came toward him.

"How's Slade?" he asked.

"He's goin' to pull through—I hope," replied Irish. "Guess all the excitement kinda shot your business."

"It sure did," agreed the bartender.

"Did Barney stay here after he reported to us about Silent?"

"Had two drinks, then went out."

"Alone?" asked Irish.

The bartender scratched the back of his neck thoughtfully.

"I think he did, but I couldn't swear to it," he finally said. "Seemed many came in for one more drink. Then they all pulled out."

"Did Dale Boyd come in for another drink?" asked Irish.

"Lemme see. No, I can't recall him comin' back after he went out with you fellows. No, I'm sure he didn't come back."

Irish nodded, turned, and headed for the hotel.

He did a lot of thinking as he went to his room, undressed, and climbed into bed.

CHAPTER SEVEN

Early the next morning Irish headed for the cafe. He was the only customer.

"Ain't you the one whose partner got knocked on the head last night?" the waitress asked.

"That's me," nodded Irish. "Things are kinda quiet this mornin'."

"Sunday," said the waitress. "What would you like?"

Irish gave his order and she went into the kitchen where he could hear her telling the cook what to prepare. He sat there, looking around. He decided it was too early to visit Doc Schulte and check on Silent.

He was nearly finished with his breakfast when Peter Benson, his head still bandaged, came into the cafe.

"How's Silent?" he asked anxiously.

"I haven't checked this morning," replied Irish. "Too early before breakfast, I thought."

"Uh-huh," nodded Peter as he sat down at the counter.

"Want some breakfast?" asked the waitress.

"Ate before I rode in," Peter replied. "Didn't know about Silent until this morning when Dale told me," he said to Irish. "That's sure too bad. Hope he'll come along all right."

"I'm sure he will," sighed Irish as he finished his eggs. "Want to walk down to Doc's with me?"

"I'd like to," nodded Peter.

Irish paid for his breakfast. Then the two of them hurried over to the Schulte home. Mrs. Schulte was sweeping the front porch as they came up. She greeted them with a big smile.

"How's Silent?" asked Irish anxiously.

"He's still unconscious," replied the woman. "Go in and see him. I think Doc's with him right now."

Irish and Peter went into Silent's bedroom. Doc was just straightening up after examining Silent's head. The bandages were off. He looked at Irish and Peter.

"Early birds," he muttered.

"How's the patient?" queried Irish.

"He's still sleeping," replied Doc. "He really took two hard blows to the head."

"He will be all right, won't he?" asked Peter.

"Oh, I'm pretty sure he will be," nodded Doc. "But you never know how long he'll be unconscious. I've seen it where a person's unconscious for a week."

"That's encouraging," snorted Irish. "Is there anything I can do?"

"Nothing." Doc shook his head. "I'll rebandage the wounds and wait. If there's any change, I'll let you know right away."

"I'll be at the hotel," said Irish as he and Peter backed out of the room.

They left the house and went over to the porch of the hotel where they sat down.

"I know this is hard on you," said Peter.

"Uh-huh, kinda lost my thinking-box," muttered Irish. "Never knew how much I depended on Silent." He paused and looked at Peter. "What are you going to do, Pete?"

"Today," smiled Peter, "Debby and I are going to church. I'll let tomorrow take care of itself. I still can't believe what that lawyer said about Uncle Jim's will."

"Did your uncle ever write you about his ranch?"

"Oh, yes, he wrote me many things about it," replied Peter. "It sounded so good."

"Did, huh?" grunted Irish. "Anything special he wrote you about, aside from cattle?"

"Oh, he told me about gold, but I believe now he was writing about the Golden Eagle Mine, which he had an interest in," replied Peter. "I asked Dale about it, and he thought that's what the old man meant. He was quite caught up in the operations of the Golden Eagle."

Irish nodded and yawned. "Didn't sleep well last night," he said as he glanced down the street where Clay Bannister was riding in. "Here comes the almighty lawyer."

Peter looked at the approaching rider and shook his head.

"I guess he's all right," he said. "Uncle Jim trusted him."

"But that will," said Irish. "It's certainly different than anyone ever suspected. Your uncle had told everyone that you were his heir. Why, he never even mentioned Annie Benson—and then this. It doesn't make sense to me."

"Nor to me," added Peter quickly.

They watched as Bannister dismounted at the Silver Coin Saloon, tied his horse, and walked over to his office. He unlocked the door and went inside.

"Wonder why he's riding so early?" queried Peter.

"Heard he spent the—"

Irish's words were cut short when Clay Bannister came running out of his office, yelling at the top of his lungs:

"Sheriff! Sheriff! Help—I've been robbed!"

Irish and Peter got to their feet as Wilbur Wendell opened his office door and looked out.

"What's the matter?" asked the sheriff.

"My office is ransacked!" wailed Bannister while Irish and Peter rushed over.

"I'll be right there," snapped Wilbur.

He went back into the office and Harry Baylor came out, buttoning his shirt. In a moment the sheriff came out, and they all went over to the lawyer's office.

"It looks like a cyclone struck here," remarked Harry.

While Peter walked off somewhere, Irish leaned against the doorway and looked the room over. Chairs

were turned over, desk drawers pulled out, and things
strewn around the place. Bannister pulled the heavy
drape back from the window so that it was easier to see
the condition of the room.

"What in hell happened?" asked the sheriff as he
stepped gingerly around things. He stopped at the desk
and looked at Bannister, who moved past him and made
a quick examination of his safe.

Then he turned and shook his head.

"At least it's all in one piece."

He crossed over to the back room. The sheriff followed him.

"Door's not locked," Bannister said to the sheriff. "I
always leave it locked. Whoever did this must have
come in the back way."

Wilbur Wendell nodded as he looked out into the
alley; then he came back past the lawyer and into the
office where he went directly to Irish.

"Wasn't Slade found out in back of this office?" he
asked.

"I don't know behind what office he was. It was just
in the alley," replied Irish. "You better ask Harry."

The sheriff nodded and turned to see Harry Baylor
just coming out of the back room with Bannister.

"Harry," said the sheriff, "where was it you found
Slade last night in the alley?"

Harry thought, shaking his head.

"In the excitement, I never paid too much attention
—and it was pitch dark out there," he replied. "Lemme
go out and take a look."

Irish followed him out the rear door. They looked

around while the sheriff stood in the doorway and watched them.

"It could have been about here," said Harry, pointing to a dark stain in the center of the alley. "Looks like blood."

"It could have been," agreed Irish as they came back into the office, with the sheriff ahead of them.

"How's Silent this mornin'?" Wilbur asked.

"Still unconscious," replied Irish.

"I dunno what he was doin' out here, but he might have bumped into the party that tore up this office," the sheriff surmised thoughtfully.

"Or he could have done it," countered Bannister.

"One remark more like that, and you'll join him at the doctor's," warned Irish.

"You don't need to threaten me," snapped Bannister.

"I'm not threatening you—I'm stating a fact," snapped Irish.

"Ease off," cautioned the sheriff as he stepped between the two. "We don't know a thing yet. Let's see what Silent has to say."

"That cowpoke would lie on a stack of Bibles," snorted the irritated lawyer.

Irish started to move past the sheriff, but Harry helped restrain him.

"Easy, Irish," cautioned Harry. "I'd like to see you settle matters, but that won't take care of things here."

Irish nodded, turned, and walked out of the office.

"I'd search Slade," said Bannister. "I don't trust him."

"You wouldn't expect him to be carryin' things with

him from here, would you?" asked Wilbur.

"He didn't have any chance to hide them, from what I heard," said the lawyer. "He probably came out of here and someone patted him over the head. If that's what happened, he'll still have them on him."

"I'll check," nodded the sheriff.

"You'd better," snapped Bannister. "Things are getting out of control in this valley, and no one's been arrested for any of the shootings."

Wilbur Wendell glared at the lawyer, spun on his heels, and tramped out of the office, not trying to avoid things on the floor. Harry followed him out to the walk.

"Well?" asked the deputy.

"I should have let Irish at him," snorted the sheriff. "Let's go see Doc and check on Silent."

They hurried to the doctor's house, to find Irish back there again, talking with Doc Schulte. Irish turned and looked at them.

"He's still unconscious," he said.

The sheriff nodded. "Irish, would you mind if we checked through his clothes?"

"Go ahead," grinned Irish. "That lawyer's going to make me mad one of these times and I'll kill him!"

They all went to the room where Silent was in bed. Quickly they went through his clothes, finding nothing pertaining to the attorney. Harry checked on his boots, but they were empty.

"Satisfy you?" asked Irish.

The sheriff nodded as they left the room and went out on the porch. Doc and Mrs. Schulte were sitting in rockers. They looked up at the men.

"I had to do it against my better judgment," said the sheriff, shaking his head. "It may keep Bannister off my neck—and Slade's."

"He better be careful what he says," warned Irish. "I don't have to take his lip even if he's one of Flat Bottom's big shots!"

"I'm with you all the way," said Harry.

The sheriff half-nodded. He knew he had to be careful in his capacity as law officer.

"Let's go back to the office and try to solve another crime," he said sarcastically.

Irish stayed on the porch with Doc and Mrs. Schulte. They watched the two officers head back to the main street.

"I'd hate to be in their shoes," said Doc. "Four murders and now this ransacking of Bannister's office."

"Uh-huh," nodded Irish. "An' don't forget the beating of Silent."

"This was such a peaceful little valley until a month ago," sighed Mrs. Schulte. "We had little business, and it was so nice."

"The worm turned," said Doc. "I've felt it coming for some time."

"Whatcha mean?" queried Irish.

"Trouble was brewing here three months ago when Bill Hansen visited the valley. He was Fred Hansen's brother—but they hated each other. Almost had a couple fights right here in town. And Bill swore that he would get even with his brother, even if it was the last thing he ever did."

"That's interesting," said Irish. "Where does this Bill Hansen live?"

"In Montana, I believe," replied Doc. "He finally left, but said that he would be back. He was pretty thick with Jim Benson and Clay Bannister. From then on, I've been waiting for things to erupt."

"Looks like they have," grunted Irish. "Wonder if this Bill Hansen is in Montana now?"

"I haven't seen him since he pulled out on the stage," replied Doc as he got to his feet. "Got to check my patient."

He went into the house and Irish looked at Mrs. Schulte. She seemed to be staring into space.

"Looking for an answer out there?" he asked softly.

She shook her head and smiled.

"I was daydreaming, I suppose," she replied. "This is the first Sunday Doc and I have missed going to church since we came here."

"I think the good Lord will excuse you under the circumstances," said Irish.

"Church should be about over by now," she said. "Suppose the reverend will drop by to check on us."

"Prob'ly," nodded Irish as he got to his feet. "I'll see how Silent is before I go back to the hotel."

He went into the house and found Doc in the hallway, a smile on his face.

"He's conscious," Doc said. "He asked for you, Irish."

Irish almost knocked Doc over as he dashed into the bedroom. Silent was propped up on several pillows. He slowly turned his head and looked at his partner.

"I figured it was you, making all that noise," he said softly.

"How you doing, pardner?"

"Could be better," replied Silent, flashing a slight smile. "What happened?"

"That's what I was going to ask you."

Silent motioned for Irish to come over closer to the bed.

"I went into Bannister's office, and when I came out, someone must have hit me over the head."

"You—you went into his office?"

"Sh-h-h!" cautioned Silent.

"What did you find out?" asked Irish. He stepped to the doorway and looked out into the hallway, but it was empty. "Doc's gone out on the porch with his wife."

"It'll keep, cowboy. I've got to get out of here."

"I know, but Doc doesn't want you wandering around for a spell," said Irish. "You take it easy, and in a couple days you'll be fine as frog's hair."

"I hope so, but tomorrow's the reading of the will," said Silent with a slight smile.

"I'll be there with Pete," said Irish.

"Tell me what you know about what happened to me," said Silent.

Irish pulled up a chair and told Silent all that he knew.

Silent listened carefully, digesting all of it. "Then the fellow that found me was murdered, eh?" He shook his head. "It sounds interesting about this Bill Hansen."

"Did you ever hear anything about him?" queried Irish.

Silent nodded but did not say anything. Sounds out in the hallway caused both men to turn and look as Peter Benson and Debby Nelson came through the doorway. They were followed by Doc and Mrs. Schulte.

"Hey, I'm sure glad to see you're awake," grinned Peter.

"So am I," said Silent. "How are you, Debby?"

"This is just terrible," sighed Debby, who was holding hands with Peter. "The minister spoke all about it this morning from the pulpit."

"Well, that's getting up in the world," said Silent. "Was everybody there at church?"

"It was a small group," replied Debby. "I don't know where most of the people were."

"Prob'ly afraid after what's been going on," said Irish.

"How long are you going to be in here?" asked Peter.

Silent turned and looked at Doc.

"He should remain another day or two," said Doc. "If he stays in bed today, perhaps by tomorrow he can get up. He'll probably be very unsteady on his feet for a day or two. That's why I want to keep him here."

"You heard the doctor," said Silent. "I wanted to be out for the reading of the will tomorrow."

"I said I'd take care of that," said Irish.

"Irish will be with me," said Peter.

"I'll be with you, too," said Debby. "Unless you don't want me."

"Oh, no, I'll want you, too," replied Peter. "Well, we must meet Debby's father. Take care, Silent. I'll see you, Irish."

The young couple turned and walked out of the room.

After they were gone and the front door was closed, Mrs. Schulte looked at Doc. "It's so nice to see Debby happy," she said.

"Wasn't she happy before Peter came?" asked Silent.

"Oh, she was—and she wasn't," the woman replied. "I never saw her tagging along with any boy before. Oh, she had some that took her to dances now and then, but nothing steady."

"Well, she selected a fine young man," said Silent. "I think I'm going to take a nap. All this talking has tired me out."

"I'll see you later," promised Irish.

Then he left the house and headed back to the hotel. He saw the lobby was empty, so he went to the cafe where he found the sheriff and deputy eating their dinner. They invited him to sit at their table.

"Just heard that Slade has regained consciousness," said Wilbur.

Irish nodded. "Yes, but he doesn't seem to know anything," he said. "He's tired and wanted to take a nap."

"I'll check with him later on to see how he got to fall down in that alley where you boys found him," said the sheriff.

"I doubt if he really knows," said Irish.

"When's Doc goin' to release him?" asked Harry.

"He said in a day or two," replied Irish. "He doesn't think Silent is able to walk very good, so he doesn't want him wandering around."

"I should say not," grunted the sheriff. "He'd make a good target for this killer person."

After Doc and Mrs. Schulte left him and closed the door, Silent leaned back on his pillows and tried to think. His head still hurt and he wished he knew who had struck him when he'd emerged from Bannister's office.

Slowly he thought over the things that Irish had told him—about Bill Hansen and his feud with his brother. Silent wondered what this had to do with the paragraph in the letter from Jim Benson that Bannister had in his desk. Then it was Peter who had mentioned to Irish that his uncle had written him about gold, but now he assumed that it was the Golden Eagle he was probably writing about. Why was that old-timer, Barney, murdered after he found Silent in the alley?

Silent pondered over these things, trying to draw something from them that would help him. He shook his head and it hurt him. He slapped his hands down on the bedding and grunted a curse. He slowly turned the sheets back and managed to sit up, his legs dangling over the edge of the bed.

He looked around and saw his clothes on the back of the chair across the room next to the wall. He wanted to get out of bed, but he was too weak.

CHAPTER EIGHT

There was quite a bit of excitement around Flat Bottom Monday morning when Clay Bannister let everyone know that at eleven o'clock the reading of the will of Jim Benson would take place in the county courthouse.

Peter Benson, Dale Boyd, Ike Jones, and Sody Smith rode in from the Box B early and had breakfast in town. Members of the Lazy N drifted into town shortly afterward, led by Debby Nelson and her father, Mike. They all met in the cafe, where the sheriff and deputy were eating.

Through the window in front, the sheriff spotted the Double D group consisting of Clyde Duggan, his son, Chuck, and Jack Harris.

"Looks like the whole county's goin' to be here," said Wilbur.

"It's a big thing," said Mike Nelson.

"An' we hope justice prevails," added Dale.

"I'll be there," said the sheriff.

"That's not what I mean, an' you know it, Wilbur," snapped Dale. "I want to see Peter get what he deserves. We all know how ol' Jim felt—and he never once mentioned a niece named Annie."

"By the way, where is this here Annie?" asked Wilbur. "I haven't seen her since she came to the hotel after church yesterday."

"Oh, she'll be around," said Harry. "Bannister will see to that."

Just then Irish came into the cafe, and they all turned their attention to him to find out about Silent.

"He's better this morning," said Irish. "In fact, he's downright ornery. He's giving Doc a hard time because he wants to attend the reading of the will, but Doc is just as stubborn and insists he stay in bed another day."

"Doc will win out," said Harry. "I know him—and I found out more'n once myself."

Irish nodded as he sat down at the counter next to Dale.

"Silent tried to get out of bed this morning and he nearly fell down," said Irish. "Those blows to the head were mighty hard. Glad he has a hard head."

"When I talked with him last night," said Wilbur, "he hadn't the faintest idea how he got back in that alley." He looked sharply at Irish. "Just how many drinks did he have Saturday night?"

"A couple," replied Irish. "That Silver Coin liquor is mighty potent."

"It must be," said Harry. "Never affected me that way."

"Silent usually doesn't take more'n one or two drinks," said Irish.

Things quieted down as they all started getting their food. The sheriff and deputy, who had come in earliest, left the cafe and went out on the walk just as Grady Halstead, Ma Halstead, and Mac Butler of the Circle H ranch rode into town in a buckboard. They waved to the two officers as they pulled up at the general store. Then Ma went into the store.

Grady Halstead was a thin, wiry rancher in his sixties. He had been in the valley for many years and owned the Circle H. He came up to the law officers and nodded.

"You'd think this was Saturday night," he said, looking around at the filled hitchracks.

"Big event," said the sheriff.

"Is it true what I heard, that ol' Jim left the ranch to his niece?"

"That's what we hear," nodded Wilbur. "In about an hour we'll know the truth about it."

"I ain't been in town for two weeks," grunted Grady. "Been down with a bad cold, so either Mac or Tige came in for mail and supplies and brought back news they heard. Got me fightin' my hat, Wilbur. I was prob'ly closer to Jim Benson than anyone else, and he never once mentioned a niece. Is she here?"

"Got in a few days ago, Grady," replied the sheriff.

"Been livin' at the hotel while young Peter Benson's been stayin' at the Box B."

"Possession's nine points o' the law," chuckled Grady.

"Yeah, in some ways," said the sheriff. "This will be settled soon and everyone can go back to their work."

"Work? Yeah, betcha that includes you, Wilbur. Reckon you've got a lot of work to do with four murders, a man beaten up, and the *eminent* attorney's office ransacked," chuckled the old rancher. Then he walked to the general store.

"Damn it!" snorted Wilbur, looking at Harry. "Yeah, we got work, but where in blazes do we start?"

"Don't ask me," said Harry Baylor. "Oh, oh, here comes trouble!"

Across the street was Clay Bannister. He came right up to the two officers.

"Sheriff, I'd like you to come with me to my office, watch me open the safe and take out the will, then escort me down to the courthouse with it," he said in a demanding tone.

"Need an extra bodyguard?" Harry asked sarcastically.

"The sheriff will do," snapped Bannister as he turned and headed back to his office.

The sheriff shrugged his shoulders and followed while the deputy stood on the walk and chuckled. Irish came out of the cafe and joined Harry.

"Somethin' happen?" asked Irish.

"Naw, that damn lawyer wants protection from the sheriff in takin' the will to the courthouse," replied

Harry. "C'mon, let's saunter down an' get a couple of good seats for this big event."

By the time they arrived, there were a few people there, and in the front row sat Annie Benson next to Neal Thompson of the Golden Eagle Mine. Irish and Harry selected seats at the rear on the aisle and relaxed. More people started to come in, and the Box B gang, with Peter, took seats across the aisle from Annie and Thompson. Soon Debby joined Peter.

By the time the sheriff and Bannister arrived, the place was really filling up with curious people from Flat Bottom. The two men went to the front and pulled up two chairs near a large table. The sheriff sat down while Bannister walked over and spoke to Annie and Thompson, ignoring Peter and his gang.

At eleven sharp, Judge Carter strode into the room, but he did not take his usual seat on the bench. He walked in front of the bench and faced the crowd. His round face beamed, and his blue eyes sparkled as he looked over the crowd.

He said, "Folks, this is rather unusual, to hold such a reading here in the local courtroom. But Mr. Bannister thought it appropriate under the circumstances, so we agreed to hold it this morning while things are quiet in the courthouse." He looked at the lawyer. "It's all yours, Mr. Bannister."

Clay Bannister got slowly to his feet and stepped up next to the judge. He drew an envelope from his pocket.

"The sheriff saw me take this out of my safe and he escorted me here with it," said Bannister with a smile as he looked the crowd over. "We will now open the envelope and take out the will."

He lifted the flap on the envelope and opened it. His eyes snapped wide as he looked into an empty envelope.

"What's the matter?" asked the sheriff, noticing the expression on the lawyer's face.

"The—the—the will," stammered Bannister, "is gone!"

"Well, I'll be darned!" snorted a voice, and all knew it was Buster Gavin with his favorite expression.

The sheriff joined Bannister and the judge as they examined the envelope.

"Are you sure it was in there?" asked the sheriff.

Bannister nodded, at a loss for words probably for the first time in his entire life.

"This is terrible," said the sheriff. "What can we do?"

"End this session right now," said the judge as he turned to the crowd. "There will be no reading of the will this morning."

Many people got up and walked out, but Peter and Debby remained with Dale in their seats. A stunned Annie Benson was in tears as Thompson tried to comfort her.

Bannister tore the envelope into pieces and let it drop to the floor while the sheriff watched him. Judge Carter turned and went back into his chambers. Irish and Harry Baylor came slowly down the aisle after the majority of the people had made their way out of the building. Irish paused next to Peter and Debby, while the deputy joined the sheriff.

"Now what?" asked Peter.

"I wish I knew," replied Irish as he glanced over at

Annie. "What a blow this must be to her."

"I feel sorry for her," said Peter. Then he turned to Debby. "I think I should go over and talk with her."

"I'll go with you," said Debby.

They went over together. The woman looked up at them.

"I'm Peter Benson. And this is Debby Nelson. You are Annie Benson."

Annie tried to smile, but the tears were running down her face. She wiped them away and nodded her head.

"This is no time to try to get friendly," snorted Neal Thompson.

"Oh?" queried Peter. "I would think it a very appropriate time."

"What business is it of yours, Mr. Thompson?" asked Debby.

"Why, Miss Benson is a friend of mine," he replied. "And this has shaken her up considerable."

"It has shaken me, too," said Peter.

He took Debby by the arm and they walked out of the courtroom, followed by Dale and Irish. Outside, they all stopped.

"Can you beat that?" grunted Peter. "I want to be friendly, but that man with Annie seemed irritated."

"What did he say?" asked Irish.

"That Miss Benson was a friend of his and that this was no time to talk with her because she was shaken up."

"That's Neal Thompson," said Dale. "Friend, huh! He hasn't known her for more than a few days."

"Perhaps," said Irish, "and again, they may have

known each other before she came here."

They all looked at Irish, who simply shrugged.

"What do you mean?" asked Peter.

"There is a possibility that Thompson may have known her in Phoenix—or some other place," explained Irish. "That's why he called her a friend."

They accepted that as they walked away from the courthouse. Just then the sheriff and deputy came out with a deflated Clay Bannister, who stopped on the walk.

"I can't imagine what happened to that will," he said for the tenth time and the officers merely grunted. "I put it in my safe after Benson signed it about three months ago."

"The safe wasn't tampered with, was it, Saturday night?" asked Wilbur as they continued walking.

Bannister shook his head.

"I don't think so," he replied. "It was the only thing in the office that wasn't thrown about." He paused and looked at the sheriff. "I still have a feeling about Slade. I think he knows more about this than he's telling."

"We'll talk with him some more," said the sheriff.

"Where was O'Day Saturday night?" asked Bannister.

"With me," said Harry Baylor quickly. "We played pool."

Bannister nodded as they came up to his office.

"I'll find out who did this to me," he said. "And when I do, there's going to be plenty of trouble."

* * *

Silent Slade was greatly amused as he listened to what had transpired at the reading of the will from Irish, Peter, Debby, and Dale.

"So Bannister was speechless, huh?" he said.

"Never saw him that way before," said Dale. "It did my heart good, but where in blazes is that will?"

"Oh, it'll show up," said Silent. "Bannister perhaps got drunk and put it somewhere else. He'll find it and everything will be settled."

"I felt sorry for that woman," said Debby. "She seemed so certain that everything would work out. When it didn't, her world seemed to collapse."

"Wonder what she will do?" asked Peter.

"Bannister will ask her to stay here a little longer," said Silent. "He can't afford to let her go back to Phoenix right now."

"Maybe she doesn't have sufficient funds to remain here," suggested Peter.

"Again Bannister will bail her out," said Silent.

"I will, will I?" snapped a voice, and they all turned to see Clay Bannister standing in the doorway, looking directly at Silent.

"If you were well, I'd slap it out of you!" he snapped, moving up to the bed. "You know where that will went!"

"Those are pretty strong words," said Silent. "If I was out of here, you wouldn't have a chance."

"Gentlemen!" snapped the doctor as he came in, followed by the sheriff. "This is no place to start a fight. My patient is not well enough to stand all these accusations."

Bannister growled something and turned to Peter.

"Get off the Box B ranch—and stay off!" he snapped.

"Why? What right do you have to tell me what to do or where to go?" snapped Peter.

"I'm executor of the will," replied Bannister. "And I want Annie Benson to move into the ranch house and take charge."

"Not so fast!" said Silent quickly. "Where's your authority, Bannister? You have no right to order Peter off the ranch or to send Annie out there."

"I don't, huh? Just you wait till I get a court order from Judge Carter," said the attorney as he turned, nearly knocking Irish over.

But the red-headed cowboy grabbed him, whirled him around, and slammed him against the wall. Bannister was stunned by the sudden move.

"Watch where you walk!" snorted Irish. "Next time I won't be so easy with you!"

Bannister edged over to the doorway and went out.

"He'll do just that," declared the sheriff. "Get a court order."

"Do you think the judge will go along with him?" asked Silent.

The sheriff shrugged his shoulders.

"I've seen him sway the old judge before," he replied. "And he might be able to do it again this time."

"Should I leave?" asked Peter. "I don't want to cause anyone any trouble."

"If you do, you'll come to the Lazy N," said Debby. "We'll fight Bannister until it's all settled."

"We'll fight him," declared Dale. "Me an' the boys will stop him from bringin' her out there."

"Take it easy," cautioned Silent. "I wish I was up so I could talk with that judge. Just watch Bannister, but be careful because we don't need any more bloodshed if we can help it." He paused and looked at Doc. "Will I be able to get out of here tomorrow?"

Doc nodded. "I'm sure you will be able to," he replied.

"When Silent gets out, watch the fur fly," grinned Irish.

Bannister went to the hotel where he found Annie and Thompson sitting in the lobby. They looked up at him.

"Well?" queried Thompson.

Bannister shrugged his shoulders.

"That Slade's no dummy," he growled. "He knows right now we haven't a leg to stand on. That will gave me all the authority. But without it, I haven't got a blasted thing but my voice."

"And that's not too good," said Thompson. "Against brains. What about Annie?"

"I'm not staying here any longer," said Annie. "I've tried to make the best of things in this hotel, but enough is enough. I'm leaving tomorrow, going back to Phoenix."

"You can't do that," Bannister protested. "I'm not made of money, and Neal helped a heck of a lot in paying for things. I'll talk with the judge and see if I can't make some arrangements for you to live at the Box B ranch."

"With those dirty-looking men?" asked Annie.

"Those are cowboys and that's the way they dress and live," said Thompson.

"It's terrible." Annie shuddered. "Even Peter Benson is getting to look like one of them."

"Perhaps you will, too," smiled Bannister. "I'll see the judge."

After he left, Thompson shook his head and looked at Annie.

"We might as well get something to eat," he suggested.

"I'm all for that," said Annie. "Come on, Neal."

As Annie and Thompson went to the cafe, they saw Irish, Peter, Debby, and Dale coming toward them from the doctor's house. The couple was seated when the four came in and took a table. At another table were Grady and Ma Halstead and Mac Butler. Debby went over to see Ma and she introduced Peter to the Circle H gang.

Dale pulled his table closer to the Halsteads' and they were able to talk and eat.

"What's goin' to happen now?" asked Grady.

"No one knows," replied Peter. "Time will tell."

"This must be a strain on you," said Ma, looking at Peter.

"It is, but things here have brightened everything up." He looked at Debby and smiled.

"I can see that," said Ma. She glanced across at Annie, then back to the men and Debby. "She doesn't look like the type that could run a ranch."

"I don't think she can," said Dale, "but Bannister is

tryin' to shove her onto us. He's goin' to try an' get a court order."

"Oh, my goodness!" Ma looked sharply at her husband. "Can he do that, Grady?"

"I dunno enough about the law, Ma," replied the old rancher. "There's so many newfangled laws today."

"I'm sure Bannister will try to pull out something new," said Irish.

"But there's always the old six-shooter law," said Dale. "If he tries to bring that gal out to the ranch, we'll greet him with hot lead."

"That's going a little far, isn't it?" asked Grady.

"What would you do if some woman was put in charge of your ranch? Someone who didn't know the first thing about a ranch, prob'ly couldn't tell a cow from a horse," growled Dale.

"I'm glad I don't have to face that situation," said Grady. "But I'd prob'ly do the same thing if it occurred."

It was evening, and the oil lamp on the table next to Silent's bed gave him enough light to manipulate the deck of cards that Doc had given him when he and Mrs. Schulte went to visit some patient out of town. Irish had been in and left.

"Darn quiet," muttered Silent as he fooled around with the cards, trying out new tricks. He was propped up in his bed, and under his pillow he had his trusty Colt .45. Irish had brought it over. He felt better with it next to him.

After a while, he put the cards on the table and blew out the lamp. He was starting to close his eyes when he thought he heard a noise: something like the snapping of a twig. His right hand went for his gun. Then he waited.

Presently the head and shoulders of a man appeared in the window as though in a framed picture. Silent watched closely. Then the moonlight glistened on the barrel of a six-shooter as it swung across the window-sill, pointing at him.

Silent, with all his strength, rolled off the bed, landing on his knees as the man outside fired. Before his second shot came, Silent returned the fire. A bullet barely missed Silent's head, and he thought he heard a groan. Then the man disappeared. Silent crawled to the window on his hands and knees, holding onto his gun. He carefully raised himself and looked out.

He could hear running footsteps fading off in the distance. Then he sank down on the floor, fingering his gun. He didn't know what it was that had warned him, but he was grateful. He pulled himself to his feet and slowly walked back to his bed and sank down. Just then the front door of the house banged open and running footsteps could be heard in the hallway. Silent lay there, his gun covering the doorway, as two men came into the room.

"Silent!" called Irish. "Silent, are you all right?"

"I'm still alive," said Silent. "Light the lamp."

The sheriff struck a match and quickly lighted the lamp. The two men looked curiously at Silent.

"What was the shootin' about?" asked Wilbur Wendell anxiously.

"Someone wanted to eliminate me," replied Silent, and he told them what had happened.

"This country's gettin' worse every day," grunted the bewildered law officer.

"How'd you escape?" asked Irish.

"I don't know, but something inside me warned me to be ready. I had my gun next to me. I'll be glad to get out of here."

"Uh-huh," nodded the sheriff. "Here you are more or less a sittin' duck."

"Where's Doc and his wife?" asked Irish.

"Doc wanted to visit a patient out somewhere, so his wife went with him," replied Silent. "Had he been here, it wouldn't have made any difference."

The sheriff nodded. "We just got back from listenin' to Bannister," he said. "An' comin' to the office, we heard the shots."

"What did Bannister have to say?" asked Silent.

"Oh, he got a court order to have Annie stay at the Box B, but the judge didn't go all the way Bannister wanted. Peter gets to stay there, too, until that will is found." He paused, shaking his head. "What happened Saturday night could be the key to where the will is."

"It could be," nodded Silent. "Wonder who popped me and then ransacked that office?"

"Wished I could answer that," said Irish. "I'd have a hunting party."

"Well, I think things are all right here now," sighed Silent. "I doubt that character will return."

"Do you think you hit him?" asked Wilbur.

"Could be," said Silent. "I heard him groan, then run away."

"We'll see if anyone reports someone shot," said Wilbur.

"I doubt if anyone connected with this affair would," said Silent. "Why they want me out of the way, I have no idea."

"Perhaps the man who hit you believes you saw who he was," suggested the sheriff.

"That could be," agreed Silent. "I wish I knew what I saw except stars."

"Well, tomorrow you should be out with the living," said Irish.

"I hope to be," laughed Silent, "but for a few moments there, I had my doubts."

CHAPTER NINE

Things were going along smoothly at the Box B
Tuesday morning when Clay Bannister drove a buggy
into the ranch yard with Annie Benson. The men had
heard of the court order and were waiting for her. Sody,
with Peter's help, had cleaned up the bedroom adjoining
Peter's, and it was ready for her.

Dale Boyd had called the group together at breakfast
and laid down the law to all of them. He said they
should treat Annie decently. And if anyone did otherwise, he would take care of them.

"Are you goin' soft?" asked Sody.

"No!" snapped Dale. "But if she is Jim's niece, we've
got to treat her with respect. She might be bossin' this

113

spread one o' these days."

So when the buggy pulled up at the front porch, Peter and Sody came out of the house, while Dale and Ike came up from the stable. Annie looked at them and then at Bannister.

"You—you mean I must live here with these things?" she asked quietly, but loud enough for Peter and Sody to hear.

"Welcome to the Box B," greeted Dale as he came up. "Ike, you an' Sody take the lady's luggage to her room."

Peter came down the steps and assisted Annie to the ground. She looked up at him. Bannister climbed down on his side and came around the rear of the buggy to where they were standing. Ike and Sody grabbed the luggage out of the buggy and carried it into the house.

"I hope you will be comfortable here," said Peter.

"Well, I've never been on a ranch before," she said softly. "It—it—"

"It's not the Palace," said Peter with a grin, "but it will grow on you, Miss Benson."

"I'd like to see my room," she said.

"Why, certainly, my dear," said Bannister, moving between Annie and Peter. "Just this way."

Peter stepped back and watched as the lawyer helped Annie up the steps, across the porch, and into the house.

"Ech," snorted Annie as she viewed the front room. It was typical room for men, and no one knew when it was last cleaned. She turned to Bannister. "You expect me to live *here?*"

"Yes," nodded Bannister. He lowered his voice. "It's

only for a short time. Then I'll take charge."

Ike and Sody came out of the bedroom, nodded to the pair, and went into the kitchen. Annie moved into the room ahead of Bannister and stopped, looking around. The room had been cleaned, the bed neatly made. And the curtains on the window were white and fresh.

"Not too bad," grunted Bannister as he looked around. "Well, what do you think of it?"

"You want the truth?" she asked.

"I don't think so," he said. "You've done nothing but complain since I picked you up at the hotel. Compromise—won't you? I'll get that will as soon as I can and all will be settled."

"You better get that will pronto!" snapped Annie. Then she went over and tested the bed with both her hands. "Not too bad."

"You'll get along fine," said Bannister. "Well, I better get back to town."

"You better!" she snapped. "Get that will!"

"Yes, yes, that's my first priority." He walked out of the bedroom.

She watched him through the open doorway as he left the house. Then she saw Peter come into the front room. He sat down on the sofa. She tossed her purse on the bed and took off a short jacket she was wearing. And she entered the front room.

Peter jumped to his feet, smiling at her.

She put her hands on her hips.

"You're from the big city," she said. "How can you stand anything like this place?"

"It'll grow on you, Miss Benson. I love it."

"Don't Miss Benson me," she snapped. "Call me Annie."

"Fine, Annie. I'm Peter."

"Why isn't this room cleaned? It looks like it hasn't been cleaned for years."

"That's a possibility," said Peter. "You see, the men who live here don't see the dirt—and spiderwebs up along the ceiling. They're content with things the way they are. Perhaps you'll be able to change things, but I doubt it."

"If I own this ranch, I'll—" She paused. "Yes, I forgot. You're also placing a claim on the Box B."

"Not a claim," said Peter. "I'm only here because my Uncle Jim asked me to come here and run the ranch for him."

"Since I came here last Friday, everything seems to be mixed up," Annie said. "If Bannister had that will, I'm sure it all would be settled."

"Perhaps," said Peter, "and again, it might not be settled."

"What do you mean by that?" she asked quickly.

"Time will tell," replied Peter. "Well, I want to take a ride. Can you ride a horse?"

"Of course not!" she snapped as Peter turned toward the door. "Wait a minute. What did you mean it might not be settled?"

"Just what I said. It might not be settled for a long, long time."

Peter walked out of the house, leaving Annie standing there, her mouth open, her eyes wide.

At the stable Peter met Dale and Ike. They glanced at him curiously.

"You look like the cat that swallowed the robin," remarked Dale.

"I'm the cat that's toying around with a robin," said Peter. "Can one of you get my horse? I'd like to ride into Flat Bottom."

Silent Slade's spirit was willing and eager, but his flesh was not. He found it difficult to get around. He was still weak but determined to leave the good doctor's house. He paid his bill and went with Irish to the hotel, stopping several times to catch his breath.

"Don't know how I'm going to get you up those stairs," grunted Irish as they entered the hotel lobby.

"Let's rest here and maybe we can figure it out," said Silent, sitting down in an overstuffed chair. "This is hell!"

"Doc said that in another day you'll be like your old self," said Irish.

"Another day—that's all he ever told me," grunted Silent. "There's work to do."

"I know, but it'll just have to wait."

"What if it can't wait?" asked Silent. "After last night's attempt on my life, I think I'm near busting things open. But I don't know just what yet. I have some ideas, and I know a few things, but there's more I don't know."

"You'll learn it all," said Irish.

"Uh-huh, if I live that long," said Silent, feeling the

bandage on his head. "Can't even wear my hat."

"Doc said he'd remove the bandage in the morning," said Irish.

Just then the hotel clerk came into the lobby.

"It's so good to see you around," he said to Silent.

"Thanks. Wish you had an elevator in this place."

The clerk glanced toward the stairs, then back to Silent.

"Perhaps Mr. O'Day and I could help you up," he suggested.

"Now that's an idea," said Irish. "C'mon, you've rested enough here. Let's try it."

Silent grunted and got to his feet, and finally he was sitting on the edge of his bed and looking longingly at his hat, which Irish had placed on the dresser.

Irish locked the door after the clerk left, then closed the window and pulled up a chair beside the bed. Silent put up his feet, making himself comfortable.

"Well?" he said. "We're alone now, so let's go over what you know."

Irish nodded as he again told his partner all he knew, trying to remember every little detail. Silent took it all in, as though he were filing it into various parts of his mind.

"I'm interested in the gold comment made by Peter," Silent said. "Do you think there could be gold on the Box B and that is why someone wants it so desperately?"

"I don't know," replied Irish. "I've talked around with the boys from the ranch. But none of them know anything about gold on the place. That's why I believe the old man had the Golden Eagle in mind."

"That could be," agreed Silent. "But we can't over-look a thing. What's Bannister up to?"

"I saw him take Annie out to the Box B just before I came to get you," replied Irish. "I don't think she ap-proved of the idea. She seemed kinda mad when they climbed into the buggy."

"I'm not too worried about that part of it right now," said Silent. "I'd like to know why Benson, King, and Hansen were murdered."

"Don't forget ol' Barney," reminded Irish. "The old fellow that found you out in the alley. By the way, what were you doing out there?"

Silent smiled as he drew up his right leg and reached down. With some effort, he removed his boot. He then pulled down his sock.

"What's undressing got to do with it?" asked Irish.

"I'm sure glad no one removed my socks," said Silent.

"They stink that bad, huh?"

"No," laughed Silent as he turned his sock inside out and the papers fell on top of the bed.

Irish leaned forward, eyes wide open.

"What in heck is that?" he asked. "Never saw you put paper in your sock. But I know you've done it in your boot when there's a hole in it. Got a hole in your old sock?"

Silent laughed as he picked up the papers.

"Here's the will," he said, handing it to Irish.

"The will?" gasped Irish. "Where did you get it, cowboy?"

"Out of Bannister's two-bit safe," replied Silent. "It's just as he said it was."

"Did you ransack his office?"

"No, that was done probably by the person who hit me on the head," replied Silent.

"What are you going to do with it?" queried Irish as he glanced at it. Then he handed it back.

"I hadn't enough time in the office Saturday night to check a few things," Silent said. "These other papers are letters that I found. Not of too much interest. One here's from Annie saying she was ready whenever Bannister needed her here. The other is a letter from Jim Benson regarding cattle shipment. But toward the end he mentioned some kind of a deal that was in the making with Bill Hansen of Montana."

"Interesting," nodded Irish.

"Yes, it's interesting, but there's something more interesting," Silent said.

He studied one of the letters carefully. Then he picked up the will and held them side by side. Next he put the will down and studied the letter, holding it up so that the light from the window was behind it.

"Light that oil lamp," he said to Irish.

"It's not dark, Silent," said Irish, but he struck a match and lighted the lamp on the nightstand.

Silent took the letter and held it up almost against the glass of the lamp. He studied the bottom of the letter very carefully. Then he nodded his head, a big smile on his face.

"Turn it off now," he said as he folded up the papers.

"Where are you going to keep those papers?" asked Irish.

"Where I had them," laughed Silent, carefully placing them inside his sock. Then he pulled on the sock and his boot.

He had no sooner finished and was stretched out on the bed when there was a knock at the door. Irish slid out of his chair, drawing his six-shooter, and moved over to the door.

"Who's there?" asked Irish.

"Me, Wilbur Wendell, the sheriff."

Irish carefully opened the door an inch and peered out. When he saw the sheriff's beaming face, he opened the door wider, replacing his gun.

Then wham! The door banged open and the sheriff was pushed into the room, knocking Irish against the wall. Before Irish or Silent knew what was going on, two masked men stepped into the room, covering them with their guns. One of the men closed the door.

"Where's the masquerade party?" asked Silent.

"Shut up!" snapped one of the men.

"Hold it!" snapped the other as he removed Irish's gun from his holster and tossed it under the bed.

The masked man nearest the bed reached down and removed Silent's gun. He pushed it under the bed with the toe of his boot.

"Now," he said, looking at the sheriff, who was sitting on the floor near the window. "Everyone will be all right if you cooperate. Otherwise, there may be a little bloodshed. And we don't want that, do we?"

He paused and looked around the room. Then he motioned for Irish to sit down next to the sheriff.

"Just sit down on the floor and keep quiet!"

Irish moved over and sat down beside the bewildered officer.

Silent sat on the bed, watching everything, studying the two masked men as best he could.

"What is it you want?" asked Silent.

"You stole that will!" accused the man by the bed. "We want it!"

"What if I don't have it?" said Silent.

"You're the only one who could have it," said the man. He turned to the other masked man. "Start searchin' this place."

While the second man went through the dresser drawers and everywhere else, Silent was amused.

"Get outa bed, you long-legged jasper," the first man snapped, motioning with his gun.

Slowly Silent stood up. The man quickly went through all of his pockets. Then he pulled the bed apart.

"Sit down an' take off your boots."

Silent sat down in a chair and removed both boots. He handed them to the masked man, who took one, then the other, and examined them.

"Where is that will!" he snarled.

"Why all the fuss over that will?" asked Silent. "I'm willing to bet that Bannister faked it."

"Huh?" gasped the bewildered sheriff, his eyes wide.

Just then the sound of voices was heard in the hallway. Someone called out for Silent.

The masked man in charge said, "Answer 'em, say

you'll be out in a minute."

Silent nodded, and called out, "We'll be out in a minute."

"Hurry up, it's Peter and the Box B boys."

The two masked men turned and backed up toward the window. One of them opened the window, and they went out fast.

Silent was on his knees seeking his gun and Irish was looking out the window. He watched the two men go to the end of the balcony, climb over the railing, and drop down. He quickly climbed out and moved to the edge. But by the time he reached the end of the balcony, they were gone. He came back as Silent moved to the window with two guns. He handed one to Irish.

"No use, they're gone," grunted Irish.

"They jumped me out in the hall," said the sheriff. "Don't you think you should let the Box B gang in?"

"There's no one there," said Silent. "I just threw my voice—and it worked."

"Well, I'll be!" gasped the officer, shaking his head. "It sure had them scared." He paused and looked curiously at Silent. "Why were they so persistent about you havin' that will?"

"Probably can't find it anywhere else so they thought I must have it," said Silent.

"Whew!" sighed the sheriff as he went to the door, unlocked it, and stepped out into the hallway. Irish followed him. The officer went toward the rear of the hallway where he found his six-shooter. "That's where they threw it," he said, coming back, shoving it into his holster.

"After all that, I think we need some nourishment," suggested Irish.

"I think I could stand something," said Silent as he came into the doorway. He locked the door and they went down the stairs, the two assisting Silent to the lobby.

The cafe was half-filled when they filed in and sat down at a table. Harry Baylor was at the counter, so he picked up his plate, glass, and silverware and joined them.

Quickly the sheriff told his deputy what had transpired up in the hotel room. Harry sat there, jaw sagging, eyes blinking.

"Shucks, I miss all the fun," he grunted.

"It wasn't fun," said Wilbur. "Those two masked gents were serious. I'm glad Silent threw his voice. That ended the little party."

"I wish I knew who they were," snorted Irish. "I'd sure make them regret the day they stepped into that room."

"We'll know soon enough," said Silent.

Irish looked at his partner and he was sure Silent knew something, but he had been with him long enough to know better than to ask him.

They were eating their meal when Peter Benson burst into the cafe and joined them.

"Sheriff, look at this note I got in the mail!" he said.

He handed a piece of paper to the law officer, who looked at it. Harry leaned in close, trying to read it.

"What's it about?" asked Silent.

"Debby," replied Peter. "Someone's going to steal

Debby if I don't go away from here."

"What does the note say?" asked Silent.

The sheriff cleared his throat and read: "'Leave Flat Bottom by midnight Monday or Debby Nelson will disappear until after you are gone. We mean business.'"

"It's not signed by anyone," added the sheriff as he looked across the table at Silent.

"Midnight Monday? Why, it's already Tuesday," said Silent.

"Uh-huh," said Peter. "No one got the mail yesterday. It was mailed here Saturday."

"Oh, oh," grunted Irish. "That doesn't sound too good."

"We'd better check the Lazy N right away," suggested Silent.

"I'm going out there now," said Peter.

"We'll ride with you," said Silent, pushing back from the table. "C'mon, Irish, get our horses. A ride might do me good."

There was little activity around the Lazy N ranch when the five riders swept into the yard through the wide gateway. The front door banged open and Mike Nelson came out on the porch, looking curiously at the men.

"Where's the war?" he asked.

"Where's Debby?" asked Peter anxiously.

"Debby?" queried the old rancher. "You didn't meet her between here an' town?"

"When did she leave here?" asked the sheriff.

"What's this all about?" asked Nelson.

Peter dismounted and walked up to the porch, handing the note to the rancher.

"Do you think someone stole Debby?" Nelson asked.

"Perhaps," said Silent. "We rode out here to check. Didn't see her on the road or in town."

Mike Nelson said:

"That's funny. She said she'd pick up the mail, go to the store, and then ride back, as she was preparin' to do some bakin' an' needed a few things."

"Well, she ain't here," said the sheriff. "Let's head back to town and see if we missed her at one of the stores."

"I'll ride with you," said Nelson. He made his way to the stable where two of his men were looking at the riders. The old man told them what he knew as he saddled his horse. They quickly threw saddles on their horses and the three of them rode out, but the five riders had already left and were heading back toward Flat Bottom.

The five riders were determined men as they galloped their horses into town. Even Silent with his head throbbing vowed to do what he could toward locating Debby Nelson. They slowed down as they entered the main street, looking at the horses at the hitchracks, but they couldn't locate   Debby's mount.

"Better check the post office an' see if she got here," said the sheriff.

Peter swung his horse in at the rack in front of the post office and quickly dismounted and entered the building. The postmaster was leaning on the counter and he squinted at Peter.

"Has Debby Nelson been in to pick up the Lazy N mail?" asked Peter.

"Haven't seen her, but I'll check their box," the man said and walked away. In a moment he returned. "Their mail is still there. Want to take it out there?"

Peter didn't answer, but whirled on his heels and ran outside where he informed the other four riders that she hadn't been there. Harry left his horse and went to the general store, but no one had seen Debby.

They were grouped in front of the sheriff's office when Mike Nelson and his two men rode in. They pulled up at the office.

"Can't locate her," said the sheriff. "Not at the post office or the general store."

"My Gawd!" gasped the old rancher, holding onto his saddle horn, his face paling. "What would they do with her?"

"Nothing," said Peter. "They want me away from here, so I'm going out to the Box B and get my things. Then I'll leave Flat Bottom."

"I reckon that's the best thing to do," said Nelson. "Who in hell has her?"

"Someone that wants Peter out of here," replied Silent. "If you have an idea, tell us, and we'll all ride out there."

The old rancher pushed his hat back on his head and squinted at the others. Then he shook his head.

"I haven't the slightest idea," he said.

"We could search each ranch," suggested the sheriff.

"I don't believe they're that dumb—to take her to a ranch," said Silent. "No, they'll stake her out somewhere while they watch Peter to see what he does."

"I'm leaving as fast as I can," said Peter.

He climbed into his saddle and swung his horse around and galloped out of town toward the Box B ranch.

"Think I'll rest for a while," said Silent. "This has been a strain after what I've been through."

"I'll ride with the sheriff, if he wants me," said Irish.

"I'll need help," nodded the sheriff. "Let's ride back toward the Lazy N and check very closely along the road to see if we can find anythin'."

Silent tied his horse to the hitchrack and went into the hotel while the rest of the group swung their horses around and started to retrace their steps.

Clay Bannister was sitting in the lobby. He looked up at Silent.

"I've been waiting for you," he said curtly.

"Too bad," grunted Silent as he sank into a chair. "You know Debby Nelson is missing?"

"She is?"

"Uh-huh, and I think you know about it," accused Silent.

"Why would I know about such a thing?"

"It's a move to get Peter Benson out of the valley, so that Annie Benson will have a better opportunity to get the Box B ranch," replied Silent. "Peter is on his way to the ranch to get his things—and leave the valley."

"Good riddance," said the lawyer.

"But you still have to produce evidence that Annie Benson is the niece of Jim Benson," said Silent. "And that isn't going to be easy."

"That's what you think," grunted Bannister, getting to his feet. "I can take care of my business."

"Like losing wills," countered Silent.

Bannister turned and walked out of the lobby.

CHAPTER TEN

Debby Nelson was riding to Flat Bottom, wondering how Peter Benson was getting along. She knew that Annie was to arrive at the ranch that morning, and she wondered what would happen. Her mind was so busy thinking about Peter that, before she realized it, two masked men had grabbed the reins of her horse.

"What's this?" asked a surprised young lady.

"You're goin' with us," replied one of the men huskily.

"But I've got to go to town," protested Debby.

"Maybe—someday," chuckled the other man as they escorted her off the road and south.

They rode for nearly a mile until they came to a

clump of trees. Here they stopped and tied Debby to her saddle. Then they blindfolded her and gagged her.

"Just be good an' nothin' will happen to you," warned one of the men.

Debby sighed and realized that there was nothing she could do. She relaxed and kept her balance as the horses started on. Where they went, she had no idea. It was a long ride and at one point they seemed to be going down a steep trail. Debby managed to brace herself against her saddle and ride it out.

After an hour or more, they halted. For the first time in a long while, she heard the men speak. But it seemed muffled and off to one side. Next she felt hands untying her bonds to the saddle, and then they helped her to the ground. A short walk brought them into what she thought was a building. But she immediately determined that it was a cave. They sat her down and tied up her hands and her feet.

"That'll hold you," said a voice. "Just sit tight. When that tenderfoot pulls out of the valley, you'll be free to go home."

Tenderfoot? They must mean Peter Benson, thought Debby. But why was Peter leaving the valley? He said he wanted to make it his home. Then it dawned on her —the problem with the Box B and the missing will. With Peter away, Annie would have a better chance at winning the ranch. Debby wished she were free so she could talk with Peter.

The sound of footsteps on gravel convinced her that she was in one of the caves along the Bubbling River at the very southern tip of the valley. She had often come there to explore. But that did not help her in her present predicament.

Annie Benson was sitting on the front porch looking the ranch over when Peter Benson returned. He left his horse at the hitchrack in front of the house and went up to the porch, looking sharply at her.

"I'd hate to be part of a kidnapping," he said. Then he went into the house.

The young woman looked puzzled. She got to her feet and followed Peter. He was busy in his room as she stepped into the doorway. He paused from removing his things from the dresser drawer and looked at her.

"What do you mean?" she asked.

"Just that—kidnapping Debby Nelson to force me to leave here, so you can claim the Box B without any opposition," he replied. Then he placed the stuff on the bed, knelt down, and pulled out his suitcase from under the bed. He opened it and began to fill it.

"I—I don't know anything about kidnapping Debby Nelson," she said.

"Well, you're a part of it, if you know it or not," said Peter. "Out here that could mean hanging to the nearest tree."

The blood drained from Annie's face, and she grasped the doorjamb for support. Just then Dale came in.

"What are you doin', Peter?" he asked.

"Leaving," replied Peter. "Someone kidnapped

Debby this morning and sent me a warning to get out of the valley, or she won't live."

"No!" gasped Dale.

"Do they hang you for kidnapping?" Annie asked Dale, taking hold of his shirt sleeve.

He looked at her and nodded.

"Yeah—if they don't kill yuh first," he replied. Then he looked back at Peter. "What's this all about, anyway?"

"Just what I told you," replied Peter. "It's a move to get me away from here, so Annie can claim this ranch."

"Oh, no!" gasped Annie, letting go of Dale's sleeve. She slowly turned, bumping into the door as she staggered around to her own room.

"Do you think she has anythin' to do with it?" asked Dale.

"Not the kidnapping," replied Peter. "But things are pointing toward a crooked deal. I'll leave, but I'll be back, you can bet on that."·

"We're all for you," said Dale. "Where will you go?"

"Right now, I don't know. Maybe stay in Custer until I hear that Debby is safe. Then I'll go on—where, I'm not sure. I liked it here."

He picked up his suitcase and walked out of the house with Dale. Sody came from the kitchen and Ike Jones from the stable, and they all met at Peter's horse.

Quickly Dale related to Ike and Sody what was happening; then he shook Peter's hand. The others also shook hands.

"You'll be back," said Sody. "We'll get the varmint that kidnapped Debby."

"I'll see you boys," Peter said as he mounted his horse and galloped out of the yard. The three men stood there watching him.

"He's all right," said Sody. "I heard him tell that female off a while ago."

"He sure as hell shook her up," said Dale. "Told her that they hung people out here for kidnappin'. It's got her fightin' her hat on what she should do."

"Yuh don't suppose she had anythin' to do with Debby's disappearance, do yuh?" asked Sody.

"Naw, she's innocent, but I believe she knows who had a hand in it," said Dale. "I'm goin' to have a little talk with that lady."

He strode into the house to find Annie standing in her doorway.

"Honest, I didn't have a thing to do with it," she said.

"Perhaps not, but you are connected with those who are behind it," said Dale. "An' the law will prove that. If yuh don't hang, yuh'll get a long term in prison for your part in this crooked deal."

"What's crooked?" asked the woman.

"Tryin' to steal this ranch—just for starts," replied Dale. "You know you're not Annie Benson. Oh, yes, prob'ly your name is Annie, but not Benson."

She went into her room, slamming the door behind her.

Buster Gavin came into the hotel just before pulling out for Custer. Seeing Silent, he stopped to talk with him.

"What's all this guff I hear about young Peter Benson an' Debby Nelson?"

"You probably heard right," said Silent. "Peter's got to leave or Debby won't come back alive."

"Well, I'll be darned!" grunted Buster. "Is he goin' out on the stage?"

"I don't know," replied Silent. "He left about an hour ago to get his suitcase, but he never mentioned how he was leaving."

"Poor guy," said Buster. "I liked the kid. Heard about that will deal. It sounds crazy to me."

"I think it is," said Silent.

"Well, I better get the stage rollin'," said Buster. "See yuh later."

He walked out of the hotel. Silent got slowly to his feet and moved over to the counter where he looked around. He saw some writing paper on a shelf, so he helped himself to it. Then he made his way up the stairs to his room. He locked the door and sat down on the edge of the bed, using the nightstand as a desk. He took a pen from the drawer and a bottle of ink, which he had placed in there when they had arrived.

"Now I'll see how good I am at writing this," he muttered. He took off his boot, removed his sock, and secured the papers. Then he sat there writing for a few minutes.

It was a couple of hours later when Irish O'Day returned to town with the sheriff and deputy. He saw Silent's horse still at the hitchrack, so he took it, with his, down to the stable.

The three men were tired after riding up and down the

length of the valley, but finding no trace of Debby Nelson. As Irish came back to the hotel, Dale, Ike, and Sody rode into town. They drew up near Irish and dismounted.

"Where's Peter?" asked Irish.

"He pulled out," replied Dale. "Left a few hours ago. Didn't you see him?"

Irish shook his head. "We was out searchin' for Debby."

"Wonder where he went," said Sody. "That young one was full o' fire when he pulled out from the ranch. Never can tell what he might do. He loved that little gal."

"You can't blame him," said Dale. "No sign of her, eh?"

"None, and we rode miles searching," replied Irish. "Whoever took her had it all planned out."

"Where's Silent?" asked Sody.

"Maybe in the hotel—I really don't know," replied Irish. "I just stabled our horses. Silent was too tired to ride, so he stayed here."

"We're goin' to have a drink, then supper," said Sody. "I left food for that gal."

"That's thoughtful of you, under the circumstances," said Irish.

"I don't believe she knew that kidnappin' was included in her deal," said Dale. "Anyway, Peter scared the livin' daylights outa her when he said that because of her part in the kidnappin' she could be hung. She asked me, so I heaped coals to the fire an' said yes, if she wasn't shot first."

"Bet she won't sleep tonight," said Irish. "Well, I'll see if I can locate Silent. Maybe see you at supper."

Irish entered the hotel while the three cowboys went to the Silver Coin Saloon. Irish found the door locked and knocked twice, paused, twice more, then once. It was a code he and Silent had. The door opened and Irish entered. Silent looked at him and Irish shrugged his shoulders.

"No trace, eh?" grunted Silent. He went back to the bed and sat down.

Irish told him what they had done, and Silent listened closely.

"Bet Wilbur's fighting his hat again," he said.

"Uh-huh, and wouldn't you, too, with all the crime committed here recently?"

"I guess I would," nodded Silent. "You know, I'm getting hungry."

"Well, let's put on the feed bag," laughed Irish. "I sure won't complain."

As Silent and Irish went to the cafe, coming from the saloon were Dale, Ike, and Sody. They all sat around a large round table and ordered their supper. As the waitress brought the food to the table, Clay Bannister came in with Jack Harris from the Double D ranch. They sat down against the wall in back of Dale and Ike. Silent was facing them.

As he ate, Silent studied the two men, letting Irish, Dale, Ike, and Sody do the talking. He was interested in Harris and watched him closely, a smile on his face.

When they finished, he stepped over to the table and spoke to Bannister.

"I believe you've got a very unhappy client," he said.

"Yes, who?" asked the lawyer.

"Annie Benson," replied Silent. "I believe she will be pulling out in the morning."

Bannister glanced quickly at Jack Harris, then up to Silent.

"What makes you think that, Slade?"

"She doesn't want to be a part in a kidnapping," replied Silent. Then he turned and walked out of the cafe.

He joined the other men on the porch of the hotel, where they were seated. It was starting to get dark, and the clerk came out and lighted the two large oil lanterns on either side of the doorway.

"Maybe we ought to head back to the ranch," said Sody. "That poor woman out there alone may go crazy with all them strange noises."

"I believe you're right," nodded Dale. "I almost forgot about her."

"Hear Peter really scared her," grinned Irish.

"He sure did," laughed Sody. "But if the shoe fits, she better get out of it fast."

"Wonder where Peter is this evenin'?" queried Dale.

"Prob'ly in Custer," grunted Sody. "He won't go too far away."

They got up and walked out to their horses. Irish and Silent sat on the hotel porch and watched them ride out of town.

At about that time, Bannister and Harris came out of

the cafe and crossed the street to the lawyer's office.

"Fine pair," grunted Irish.

"Like an ostrich," grunted Silent. "Hide your head and think you're all hidden."

"Oho!" chuckled Irish. "I think I know what you mean, cowboy."

Silent felt his head and looked sideways at Irish.

"Be glad to get this white wrapping off my head. Without a hat, I make a good target that you can see in the dark," Silent said.

"Yeah, by golly, you sure do," nodded Irish. "What do you suggest we do?"

"Better go up to our room," said Silent, getting to his feet. "I think it will be much safer. Perhaps in the morning Doc will take the bandage off."

Before anyone appeared on the main street of Flat Bottom, Mike Nelson and his two hired hands, Hop Porter and Al Swift, rode into town. They stopped in front of the sheriff's office. Nelson swung down from his saddle and knocked loudly on the office door.

After several hard knocks, the door opened slightly, and a blurry-eyed Harry Baylor peered out.

"Whatsa matter?" he muttered.

"Debby hasn't come home," replied Mike Nelson.

"You're wakin' me an' Wilbur up to tell us that?" snorted the deputy. "Man, look at the time. No one's up around here yet."

"We've been up all night," said Nelson.

Just then Wilbur Wendell appeared in the doorway,

shoving Harry into the background. He squinted at Nelson, then at his two riders.

"We did all we could yesterday," said the sheriff as he hitched up his suspenders. "We'll be out soon, Mike."

"You better be!" snorted the old rancher. He turned and walked out to his men. "Let's get breakfast here. Then we'll ride!"

They tramped into the cafe where only the waitress was visible, but they could hear pots and pans banging together in the kitchen. They sat at a table by the large front window and ordered their meal.

They were nearly through when the sheriff and his deputy came into the cafe, closely followed by Silent and Irish. The four of them took a table near Nelson and his men.

"Up early, ain'tcha?" Irish asked the officers.

"Uh-huh," yawned the sheriff. "Poundin' on your door can interrupt a good sleep."

"Who pounded on your door?" asked Silent.

"Mike Nelson," replied the sheriff, glancing over at the rancher. "Came to say that Debby never returned last night."

"An' Peter Benson pulled out," added Harry. "They said they'd turn her loose when he was gone."

"Probably watched Peter to see where he went," said Silent, and he lowered his voice. "There's a chance that she saw who kidnapped her."

"Oh, no!" gasped the sheriff. "They'd never turn her loose if she knew who they were."

Silent nodded and leaned back.

"That's one reason; the other is that they will watch Peter for a day or two to see if he pulls entirely out of the country."

"Uh-huh," nodded Wilbur. "Good gosh, who kidnapped her?"

"That's a good question," grunted Silent. "And I think those two masked men who came to our hotel room are connected with it."

"Do you think it has anythin' to do with the murders?" asked Harry.

Silent nodded. "Right now I think it does, but by tonight, who knows?"

"I hate these things," sighed the sheriff as he pushed himself back from the table. He looked over at Mike Nelson. Nelson had finished and was waiting for the officers to make the first move.

"We'll start in ridin' again," sighed Harry. "Want to join us?"

"I've got to see Doc and pray he takes off these bandages," said Silent. "Irish can ride if he cares to."

"I'll ride, if it's all right with you, Silent."

"Go ahead. No use sitting around here with an old man," said Silent.

They got to their feet and walked over to Nelson's table.

"We'll all ride, except Slade," said the sheriff. "He's got to see the Doc this mornin'."

It didn't take them long to saddle up and head out of town. Silent watched them, wishing he was with them. But he knew he had things to do. He walked down to

Doc Schulte's house and found the doctor and his wife having breakfast.

"Care to join us?" asked Doc.

Silent shook his head. "Just finished, Doc, but thanks, anyway. Thought later you could get this white turban off my head."

"We'll do that," nodded Doc. "Let me finish."

After Silent sat down, and Mrs. Schulte insisted on giving him a cup of coffee, the doctor spoke up:

"What's the latest excitement around Flat Bottom?"

"Debby Nelson hasn't showed up," replied Silent. "A posse is out riding around looking for her."

"Think they'll find her?" asked Doc.

Silent shook his head. "They hid her so that no one will find her," he replied. "Peter's gone, though, so they should release her."

"I wouldn't trust anyone who did such a thing," remarked Mrs. Schulte.

"Neither would I," nodded Silent.

Doc finished eating and took Silent into the bedroom where he had stayed. Doc carefully removed the bandage and examined the wounds.

"Not bad," he grunted. "Mother's idea and salve sure worked great. It's pulled together. Now, if you'll be careful with your hat, you can get along fine."

"I'll be careful—not even tip it to a woman," grinned Silent as he felt his head. "Wasn't sure it was all there."

"Any pain?"

"Nope," replied Silent. "That salve must have really worked."

Doc nodded as he turned and walked out of the room. Silent got to his feet and followed him into the front room. There Doc went to the desk and opened the drawer and took out the cigar box. He picked up a tagged bullet, turned, and looked at Silent.

"Thought you'd like to see this bullet. It came from ol' Barney."

Silent moved in and took the bullet. He looked at it closely. There was the same scratch on it as on the other three bullets.

"Fired from the same gun," he said.

Doc nodded. "I watched you the other day and saw what you meant when you told the sheriff that bullets talked. I saw that scratch on the others, so I looked at this one. Must have been the same killer, eh?"

"It could be," nodded Silent, "and again, that gun could be used for murder by whoever wanted to commit the act within a gang."

"I never thought of that," sighed Doc.

"What happened to Barney's body?"

"We buried it yesterday morning," replied Doc. "He had no one, so I took care of it."

"I'll donate toward it," said Silent. "No telling what would have happened to me if he hadn't found me."

He dug into his pocket, brought out some currency, and handed it to Doc.

"You don't have to do that," said Doc.

"I insist," grinned Silent. "Now I've got to get my hat and see how it fits."

He turned and walked out of the doctor's house with more knowledge to add to his collection.

* * *

"I don't care what she says. I'm not takin' any orders from her," snapped Sody Smith as he stood in the open doorway of the Box B stable and looked at Dale and Ike. "No sir, she can't boss me around."

"I agree," nodded Dale. "I'll have a talk with her."

"You better, or you'll have to depend on *her* cookin' —an' I doubt if she knows how to boil water."

Dale nodded and smiled as he headed for the ranch house. Ike moved in next to Sody. They watched the foreman enter the kitchen door.

"I don't like her," declared Ike. "She thinks she's a goddess."

"I don't think Dale will be able to tame her," grunted Sody. "Imagine tryin' to tell me how to make apple pie?"

"She ain't never ate any o' your pie," said Ike. "It's the best ever."

"Thank yuh, Ike," grinned Sody. "First good words I've heard today. Hope Dale puts her in her place."

Dale found Annie in the front room, sprawled on the sofa, a pillow beneath her red silky hair. She looked at him curiously as he came from the kitchen, his hat held in his right hand. He stopped and looked down at her.

"It's that darn cook, isn't it?" she snapped at him.

"Sody's the best ranch cook in the county," said Dale quietly. "He has charge of the kitchen, and no one interferes with him."

"Well, I'll tell him what I think! I'm running this ranch!"

"Not yet," countered Dale. "There are some legal details to be ironed out before you know *if* you own this spread or not."

"I own it!" she snapped as she sat up. "I don't need any of your two-bit advice."

"Well, if you feel that way, perhaps I shall get Bannister and have him take you back to Flat Bottom," said Dale. And he started for the kitchen door.

"Wait a minute!" she snapped.

He stopped, turned, and looked at her.

"What do you want—to give me more orders?" he shouted.

"No, I just don't want you to tell Bannister," she said. "I guess I'm a little on edge right now."

"Well, relax and enjoy your life," said Dale. "It might not last too long."

He walked out, leaving her there with her jaw sagging and her eyes blinking.

As Dale rounded the side of the house, he saw a horseman approach, so he stopped and waited. It was Silent Slade. He drew up and dismounted at the hitchrack in front. Dale came up as he tied off his horse.

"How you feelin'?" asked Dale, noticing that Silent again wore his hat.

"Head's better," replied Silent. "Doc removed the bandages. I feel ten pounds lighter."

"What brings you out here?" asked Dale.

"Did Peter say anything to you about where he was going when he rode away yesterday?"

Dale thought, then shook his head.

"Come to think of it, no. He just said he was leavin'

the country because of Debby Nelson being kidnapped. Did they release her?"

"Nope—at least not an hour or so ago," replied Silent. "I was wondering just where Peter went. Perhaps some of the gang followed him to see that he went away. If he stayed in Custer, they may wait until he pulls completely out of the country."

Dale nodded.

"This is one hell of a mess, Silent," he said thoughtfully. "This Annie woman doesn't deserve this ranch. It really belongs to Peter, but how can we straighten such a thing out?"

"How is she doing here?"

"Terrible! Bossin' everyone. Even ol' Sody threatened to pull out," replied Dale. "She's a terror—like a spoiled kid."

"What's she doing now?" asked Silent.

"I just left her in the front room layin' on the sofa. Why?"

"Check and see if she's still there," said Silent. "I've got an idea that might work."

"Anythin' is worth a try," said Dale. He went up on the porch and looked into the front room.

"She's gone to her room. The door's closed," he said, turning to Silent.

"Her room's the first on the left side rear, isn't it?"

"Uh-huh, why?"

"Leave it to me. You go down to the stable and get the buckboard ready to take her into town."

"How do you know she'll leave?"

"Just leave that to me, will you?"

Dale started toward the stable while Silent made his way around the house to the rear. There were several poplar trees close to the house, giving plenty of shade. He moved cautiously along the wall to the window. It was open and the curtain was pulled back. He peeked in and saw Annie stretched out on her bed. Her eyes were closed.

He leaned against the wall, thinking carefully. Then he began.

"Annie—Annie," he said, throwing his voice into the room. He peeked through the window to see her reaction.

Annie sat up on the bed, as though moved by a spring. She looked all around but didn't see anyone, so she started to lie back down, thinking that she had fallen asleep and dreamed someone was calling her.

"Annie," said Silent again.

She sprang up again, a frown on her forehead. The door was closed, and no one was around.

"Annie—I know you hear me," said Silent.

"Who are you? Where are you?"

"I'm beside your bed," replied the voice. "I am Jim Benson. Don't you recognize *your uncle's* voice?"

She gasped, eyes wide as her hands grasped the blanket on top of the bed.

"You—you, oh, no! There isn't such a thing as ghosts! Who's playing this trick on me? Where are you."

"I'm right here, Annie," said Silent. "Do you want me to touch you?"

"Oh, no!" she gasped, pulling the blanket around her.

"That blanket is no protection against me," said Silent slowly. "I can bring you over to my side should I want to. It's not too bad over here, no crooks."

Annie's eyes blinked, grew wide again as she looked around, trying in her mind to picture Jim Benson.

"Why—why did you—you come back here?" asked Annie slowly.

"Because I left my ranch to my nephew Peter Benson—not you. In fact, I know your name is not Benson. You are an imposter, and if the law doesn't take care of you, I will."

"What'll you do?" she asked anxiously.

"Kill you," replied the voice. "You had me killed, so you could get this ranch. You knew that somewhere on this ranch there is gold."

Silent paused and watched her closely. She was half-turned away from the window, still clutching the blanket around her.

"I—I never killed you," she said. "I came way after you were dead."

"Yes, but you knew what was going to happen," said Silent slowly. "You were told in Phoenix when Clay Bannister visited with you. Oh, what a time you two had over there!"

"How'd you know?" she asked quickly.

"I know everything," replied Silent. "You're implicated in the kidnapping of Debby Nelson. You have walked right into a long, hard prison term, and I won't be at peace with my maker until I see that justice is done to you, to Bannister, and to the men who worked for him."

With that, Silent slipped away and headed back toward the front of the ranch.

Annie looked around, shaking her head. Tears came into her blue eyes and she slowly wiped them away. Then she swung her legs off the bed and got slowly to her feet. She walked around the room, her hands stretched out in front of her like a sleep walker's. She investigated every part of the room, but found nothing. She finally opened the door and looked out into an empty front room.

Annie Benson sighed deeply, wiped some more tears away, and shook her head. What was she going to do? No one would believe it if she said that Jim Benson's ghost had talked to her. She turned and looked back into the room.

"Are you still here?" she asked loudly enough to bring Sody from the kitchen into the front room.

"Were you callin' me?" he asked.

"Oh, no, no," she replied as she stepped back into her room and closed the door.

Sody looked after her, shook his head and went back into the kitchen just as Silent and Dale walked in the rear door.

"Hey, that gal's loco," announced the ranch cook.

"What do yuh mean?" asked Dale.

"She's talkin' to someone—only, no one's around," said Sody, shaking his head.

"That's serious," said Dale. "What do you think about it, Silent?"

"She probably thinks she heard someone," said

Silent. "Happens lots of time to persons under the stress she's been under."

"Uh-huh," nodded Dale as he went into the front room. He could hear sounds in her bedroom. Then the door opened and Annie looked out.

"Oh, Dale, will you please take me into town?" she asked.

"Why, sure," nodded Dale. "When do you want to go?"

"Just as soon as possible. I'll have my suitcases ready in a minute!"

CHAPTER ELEVEN

Peter Benson awoke in his hotel room in Custer. He climbed out of bed, quickly dressed, and went down the street to a cafe where he had a good breakfast. All the time, he was wondering if Debby Nelson had been brought back home. Deep down inside him, he felt that the people who had kidnapped her were not going to keep their word.

He was tempted to return to Flat Bottom and face whoever was trying to take over the Box B ranch. Sitting down on the porch in front of the general store, he wondered what was going on in the valley. He kept wondering for several hours.

The stage from Flat Bottom finally came down the

main street on its way to the livery stable at the farther end of town. Peter got to his feet, hitched up his gun belt and walked to the livery stable. Buster Gavin, who was unharnessing the team, looked sharply at Peter.

"Well, I'll be darned!" he grunted, stopping his work. "What in blazes are you doin' here?"

"Trying to figure out what to do, Buster," said Peter. "Do you know if Debby Nelson is back home yet?"

Buster shook his head. "When I left, she wasn't home. A posse was out searchin' for her."

"Blasted liars!" snorted Peter.

"Who?"

"The ones that kidnapped her. They said they'd let her go if I left the valley. Well, I left."

Buster nodded. "Can't trust kidnappers," he said.

"That's what I'm finding out," said Peter. "It's the first time I was ever connected with a kidnapping."

"An' you're pretty sweet on Debby, ain'tcha, Peter?" asked Buster.

"Yes, I suppose I am," he replied. "She's the nicest girl I ever met."

"Uh-huh," nodded Buster. "You gave up a chance to own the finest ranch in order to save her life, eh? Well, I'll be darned! What'll you do now?"

"Right now I think I'll get my horse and take a little ride."

"Be careful," warned Buster. "Them kidnappers might be watchin' yuh."

"You think so?" asked Peter. Buster nodded. "I've kept my eyes open, but I haven't seen anyone familiar."

"You don't know who they are," said Buster. "Just be

careful, Pete. I kinda like yuh an' I'd hate to see yuh killed."

"Thanks a lot," said Peter as he entered the livery stable to get his horse.

Peter rode his horse out of Custer, going west. But after a while, he drew up at the side of the road and waited. No one appeared, so he swung around and carefully circled Custer. And a short time later he made his way up to the main road leading to Flat Bottom.

"Perhaps I'm a dumb fool," he told his horse. "But I have to go back. Debby needs me."

He rode along, traveling at a walk, and he studied the countryside. It looked different from the way it had inside that rocking stage. Finally he located the spot where the two bodies had lain. He paused and looked around, shaking his head. Then he rode on to the rim of the mesa where he pulled off the road.

Far below the mesa was a narrow, winding canyon with the Bubbling River running through it. Peter could even see a narrow trail down there.

Presently he saw a lone rider appear out of nowhere and start moving toward Flat Bottom.

"What's he doing down there?" Peter asked aloud. He studied the canyon more closely now and saw that what appeared to be caves were located on the other side of the river.

Peter swung his horse around and went back to the main road, then started down into the valley. At times he could see the man below him in the canyon and he wondered who he was and what he was doing there alone.

Peter's eyes then spotted a trail leading off the road

and down the side of the canyon. He rode over to it, and he saw it intersected the trail down below. He carefully urged the horse down this trail. It was narrow and one mistake would be the last one for both horse and rider.

As they went deeper into the canyon, the sun began to disappear from view, and purple and gold shadows seemed to be dancing on the rocks. But he kept going. Once in a while he saw the man up ahead, but the man was going away from where Peter was. He apparently had not seen Peter coming down into the canyon.

On the far side of the chasm the colors were magnificent. But Peter had no eyes for the beauty of the sunset. As he reached the bottom of the canyon, Peter looked around. Across the river he could see some large boulders, and there was a deep crevice. And also some well-concealed caves.

"That man must have come from there," he said to himself as his eyes turned to the river, which was about twenty feet across. He wondered how deep it was.

Peter was an excellent swimmer, but he had never swum with his clothes on. He started to dismount when he saw a figure emerge from the crevice and stop by a boulder. The person stood there, looking up the trail in the direction the rider had taken.

"What's he doing down here?" Peter asked aloud.

The person turned and went back into the crevice. Peter thought for a moment and made a decision. That must be one of the kidnappers and Debby must be back near that crevice, too. How many men were there with her? He looked again at the river. He knew he would have to get across it. He felt the butt of his six-shooter and smiled. Then he carefully drew out the gun and checked it. It was loaded.

Peter started south along the river, seeking a better-looking place to cross. He rode slowly. Suddenly he drew up the reins. His eyes had spotted a sandbar that spanned the river only a few feet below the surface. He dismounted and walked into the water, holding onto his reins, leading his horse, which balked for a moment. But Peter jerked on the reins, so the horse reluctantly followed.

As it turned out, the water was only about three feet deep. When they got to the other side, Peter petted the horse; then he pulled off his boots, emptied out the water, and donned them again. He mounted and started along the trail toward the crevice. It would soon be dark, but enough light came from above to show him the way.

Suddenly Peter felt a tug at his leg. The horse seemed to fairly fall from under him, while the crash of a shot echoed back and forth from the sides of the canyon. Peter sprawled above his horse, which slid down toward the water. He pulled his gun from his holster and looked around. For several moments he did not move. But his eyes were searching for the shooter.

Then Peter slowly drew up his left leg. The bullet had scored him slightly just above the kneecap, doing little damage. He looked down at his horse, which did not move.

Peter turned over on his back, twisting sideways, try-ing to see ahead of him. He could see nobody. Ignor-antly inviting another shot, he got to his feet and stepped past his horse to the edge of the river.

Another shot crashed out, the bullet passing close to Peter. His feet flew out from under him, and he almost pitched into the river. But he scrambled away from the water and started crawling along beside it, protected by brush and rocks. He finally came to a small opening where he sat down and checked himself over. He was uninjured except for some cuts and bruises.

But he clung to his six-shooter. Then he got on his knees, partly hidden by a large mesquite clump.

In fact, he was so well hidden by the mesquite that the man above, holding a rifle ready, did not see him. The man paused, looking around. Then he lifted the rifle, pointed it in Peter's general direction, and pulled the trigger.

The bullet crashed into the brush just in back of where Peter had been. He saw the man did not know exactly where he was and was firing somewhat blindly in hopes of hitting him. Peter lifted his gun slowly until he was sure he could hit the man, and he pulled the trigger.

The man dropped backward, his rifle clattering on the hard trail. He let out a yelp of amazement.

"I guess I didn't kill him," said Peter, and he began to angle his way around the mesquite to a large boulder. He saw another boulder farther on. It seemed to beckon him, but another bullet struck just short of him, cutting his right cheek with flying gravel. Peter curled up behind the first boulder and took stock of the situation.

This won't do, he decided. I'm doing all the moving. If I could get to that other boulder, I could crawl up the side and be on a level with him. And I'd have a better chance to get him.

So Peter moved toward the other boulder, trying to ignore the bullets fired by his adversary. By the time he had reached the big rock and gotten a good look at the other man, the other man had spotted him.

Both men fired. But Peter's aim was better. It was apparent he had killed his opponent.

Peter did not go near the body. He sighed heavily and headed for the crevice, where he now saw two horses. And on one side of the crevice was a cave. He moved toward the cave. It was pitch dark inside, so he got a match and struck it on his boot sole.

In the faint light Peter saw a figure huddled against the cave wall.

"Ouch!" The match burned his fingers, and he dropped it. But he moved forward, feeling his way until he bumped into the figure. He quickly knelt down then.

"Debby, is that you?" he asked.

There was a mumble, but that was all. He lit another match and saw it was Debby, her eyes blindfolded, her mouth gagged, her arms and legs tied together. In the dark, Peter worked as fast as his tired fingers could, taking off the blindfold, then the gag.

"Are you all right, darling?" he asked eagerly as he began loosening the ropes around her hands.

"You—you came," she panted hoarsely. "Oh, Peter."

"Don't try to talk right now," he said as he pulled the ropes off her legs. "Do you think you can walk? We've got to get out of here—it's getting dark."

"I—I'll make it with you," she replied slowly.

He helped Debby to her feet, and she nearly collapsed. But he grabbed her.

"Easy does it," he said. "There's horses outside this cave."

He assisted her slowly out to the horses and, with some effort, managed to get her into the saddle of the nearest one.

"Can you ride all right?" he asked.

"I can," she replied as he mounted the other horse. "I know the way out of here. I've been here many times. It's not too far to the Lazy N."

Dale Boyd dropped Annie Benson and her baggage at the hotel. Then he walked across the street to the law office of Clay Bannister. He found the attorney talking with a stranger. Boyd paused just inside the door as Bannister glanced at him.

"What do you want, Boyd?" Bannister asked.

"I just brought Annie Benson into town, and she's goin' to stay at the hotel," replied Dale.

"Annie in town? Why?"

"I think she's gone loco," said Dale. "She kept talkin' about her holdin' a conversation with Jim Benson's ghost."

"Bosh!" grunted Bannister. "Talking with a ghost! How crazy can you get?"

"You'd better find out before she goes to the sheriff with her tale of woe," said Dale. "I told her to talk with you first."

Bannister nodded and turned to the stranger.

"Sorry this had to come up, Bill, but it's most important to all of us that I talk with Annie Benson right now."

"Go ahead, don't mind me. I'll be here for a few days," replied the stranger called Bill.

He and the lawyer followed Dale out of the office. Bannister locked the door while Dale started for the Silver Coin Saloon. Bannister and the stranger headed for the hotel. They had just stepped into the lobby when Silent came around the corner from the livery stable and saw Dale, who paused, waving for Silent to join him.

"Brought Annie Benson in, eh?" said Silent.

"Yes, I did."

"How did she take the trip?"

"Seems like she's crazy," replied Dale. "What did you do to her?"

"Nothing," replied Silent with a smile. "Perhaps her conscience is taking hold of her."

"Somethin' sure did," said Dale. "Bannister is over there with her at the hotel. Have a drink?"

"Not now," replied Silent, "but thanks, anyway. I want to check to see how things are around town."

Silent walked down to the general store where he saw Buster Gavin buying some things at the counter. He waited until the stage driver stepped out of the store.

"How's your head?" asked Buster.

"Getting along," replied Silent. "Did you see Peter Benson in Custer?"

"Sure did," nodded the stage driver. "He was moonin' around the place. Then he got his horse and rode away. He asked me if Debby Nelson had been turned loose and he was upset when he found out that she hadn't been."

"Wonder where he went?" queried Silent. "I thought he might stay in Custer for a few days. Anything exciting happening there?"

"Same ol' dead place," replied Buster. "Had me a payin' customer comin' over here."

"Male or female?"

"Man," replied Buster. "Don't think you know him. It's Bill Hansen. He's brother to the Hansen that was murdered last week. He said he'd be here for a week or two. After he piled his goods in at the hotel, he went to Bannister's office. They was pretty close when he was here before."

Silent nodded as his mind flashed back to the letter he had found in Bannister's desk. Just then a rider swung into town and pulled up in front of Bannister's office, dismounted, tied his reins, and went to the door. But he found it locked.

Silent and Buster looked at the figure across the street. It was too dark to tell who it was until he walked over to the saloon.

"Chuck Duggan," muttered Buster. "Seems everyone wants Bannister."

"Perhaps Bannister does the law work for the Double D ranch," suggested Silent.

"I'd be darned if I'd have him," grunted the old-timer. "Well, gotta get back to the stable with these things for Emory." Buster hurried away.

Silent had started for the hotel when he heard the clatter of several horses on the street. Turning, he saw part of the sheriff's posse riding into Flat Bottom. Wilbur, Harry, and Irish pulled up in front of the sheriff's office.

"You look beat," said Silent as he walked up to them.

"The darkness hides a lot of it," grunted Irish. "Well, I sure learned a lot about this valley."

"Fruitless?" asked Silent.

"You can say that," nodded the sheriff as he hitched up his belt. "We rode back and forth across this valley and visited every ranch."

"An' not a trace o' Debby," added Harry disgustedly. "They sure got her hid somewheres."

"Where's the Lazy N boys?" asked Silent.

"We left them at their ranch house," replied Irish. "No use their riding into town an' then back."

"I suggest we all eat," said Wilbur. "Haven't sat down to a meal since breakfast."

They entered the cafe, found a table, and quickly placed their orders. The other three questioned Silent about the activity in town.

"If you call the arrival of Bill Hansen excitement, then there was some," he said.

"Bill Hansen here again?" queried the sheriff. "Wonder what brought him here?"

"Probably Bannister," replied Silent. "Hansen's been with the lawyer ever since he arrived, I heard."

"I heard they was tryin' to put a deal together with Jim Benson regardin' the Box B ranch," said Harry.

"Maybe Bill thinks he can get it now that Jim is dead."

"Nothin' can be done until that will is found," said the sheriff.

"It might pop up anytime," said Silent. "You never can tell."

CHAPTER TWELVE

Silent Slade and Irish O'Day spent the early evening around town, looking into the stores, the hotel, and the saloon. They saw Annie Benson go from the cafe to the hotel and up to her room. Buster Gavin and Emory Hill came from the livery stable and went to the Silver Coin Saloon.

Silent and Irish stopped in front of the saloon and looked inside. Buster and Emory were at the bar with several men. At the poker table to the left of the door were Clay Bannister, Neal Thompson, Bill Hansen, Clyde Duggan, and young Chuck Duggan. They were not playing cards, just drinking and talking.

"Shall we go in and have a snort?" asked Irish.

"We might as well," replied Silent. "Things are too quiet."

A rider suddenly came galloping down the main street and stopped in front of the sheriff's office. Silent and Irish turned and looked as the man slid out of his saddle.

"Peter!" snapped Silent when he saw the man in the lamp light from the office. "C'mon!"

They ran across the street just in time to hear Peter blurt out:

"Debby's at the Lazy N!"

The sheriff was seated at his desk, and Harry was sitting on his cot, both looking intently at Peter Benson as Silent and Irish stepped into the doorway.

"Are you sure of that?" asked the sheriff.

"Uh-huh," nodded Peter. "I found her in a cave."

"You found her?" asked Silent, studying Peter.

The young man's face had been cleaned, but the bruises still showed, and his clothes were torn, one leg in shreds.

Peter quickly told them what had taken place, trying to remember all the details.

"Who'd you shoot?" asked Irish.

"I don't know," replied Peter. "I never looked. It was getting dark and I wanted to get out of there."

"Was he dead?" asked the sheriff.

"I was pretty sure he was," replied Peter. "What an experience!"

"Is Debby all right?" asked Silent.

Peter nodded. "A lot better off than I am. They cleaned me up before I headed in here. Mr. Nelson said they'd be coming in shortly."

"What do you make of it, Silent?" asked the sheriff.

"I think it's about time for a showdown. I have a little plan, but I'm going to need all your cooperation."

"We'll help you," said Harry as he got to his feet.

"What's your plan?" queried Wilbur anxiously.

"You'll see." Silent paused. "Do you have a pencil and paper?"

The sheriff produced both and Silent bent over the desk, quickly sketching the floor plan of the saloon. He marked the bar and the various tables and put a big "X" on the one where Bannister and the others were seated.

"Now," he said, with everyone watching him. "Sheriff, I want you to go around behind that poker table, possibly ten to fifteen feet from it, and keep your eyes open. Harry, I want to you stay on this side of the door, just inside, and, Irish, you stand on the other side of the door. Watch everything." He paused and looked at Peter. "You watch from outside. When you see me raise my right hand and push my hat back on my head, you walk into the room, stop about halfway between the door and the table."

"What's goin' to happen?" asked Wilbur.

"I'm not quite sure," replied Silent, straightening up. "But I'll guarantee you it'll be very interesting. Now give me five minutes, as I've got to get something from our hotel room. Then we move in."

"This sounds exciting," Peter said.

"Nothing like you've been through," Silent told him, then walked out of the office.

"Is he like this often?" asked Harry.

"Just now and then—and that's the time you loosen your six-shooter and keep alert," replied Irish.

He moved to the doorway just as riders came down the street and pulled in at the hitchrack. In the dark he could see four riders—Debby, Mike, and two Lazy N hands. They crowded into the office, everyone speaking. Peter took Debby by the arm and led her to the rear of the room, talking seriously with her. Then they came back to the front.

"It's about time to move," said Irish.

"What's doin'?" asked Nelson.

"Silent plans a showdown of some kind," replied Wilbur.

"What can we do?" asked the old rancher.

"Might as well come with us," said Harry.

"Debby, you better stay here," cautioned Irish. "There could be some shooting."

She looked at Peter. He smiled and nodded, so she went back into the office as the men crossed the street. Silent was coming out of the hotel, a piece of paper in one hand. He joined them at the saloon entrance, glancing at Nelson and his two men.

"The more the merrier," Silent said. "Nelson, you and your men move in first and go to the bar, but don't pay any attention to the group at the poker table until I start to speak."

"C'mon, boys," snapped Nelson, and they entered the saloon.

"Now each of you know where to go?" queried Silent.

They all nodded, and the sheriff and deputy sauntered

into the saloon. Irish followed them.

Silent looked at Peter. "Are you ready?" he asked.

"As much as I'll ever be."

Silent walked into the room, paused just inside, and looked around. Then he moved toward the poker table where the five men sat. He stopped behind Chuck Duggan, and Bannister looked up to see him.

"This isn't a poker game," the lawyer said.

"I see that," said Silent. "New deck of cards here isn't being used."

Before they knew what was going on, he stepped between the two Duggans, reached out with his right hand, and picked up the deck. They all looked curiously at him as he pushed the piece of paper he'd been holding into his hip pocket and carefully removed the cards from the box, turning them over in his fingers.

"Never seen a new deck of cards before?" queried Bannister.

"Not one like these," replied Silent as he manipulated them in his fingers and split them carefully. Then with the deck back together, he tapped them on the top.

"Gents, let me show you what I mean," Silent said as he leaned forward and quickly dealt the cards out, first to Bannister, and then around the table. The cards fell face up. Bannister got the ace of spades, Thompson, the king of spades, Hansen, the queen of spades, Clyde Duggan, the jack of spades, and Chuck Duggan, the ten of spades. The men looked curiously from their cards to Silent.

"What's the meaning of all this?" demanded Thompson.

"What do you see before you?" asked Silent.

"Spades!" snorted Thompson. "All spades!"

"That's right," nodded Silent. "And what color are spades?"

"Black," replied Thompson. "So what?"

"Black stands for death," replied Silent as his eyes took in the five men before him. He moved a step back, looking directly at Bannister.

"You know and I know," Silent said evenly, "the game's played out."

"What's all this hocus-pocus about?" demanded Hansen as he pushed his chair back from the table.

"That's all it is," grunted Bannister. "This cowboy thinks he's so bloody smart. Don't listen to him."

"No, don't listen to me," said Silent. "I've got a lot of interesting answers to questions that have buffaloed the law for some time."

Thompson glanced sharply at Bannister. Then he pushed his chair away from the table. The two Duggans sat there, unable to move back because Silent was directly behind them.

Bannister licked his lips nervously as he squinted up at Silent, wondering what the man really had on his mind.

"I have some information for all of you," said Silent, loud enough so everyone in the room could hear. "Debby Nelson was returned to her home this evening and is now here in town."

Those words shocked the five men, and the two Duggans glanced quickly at each other, then at Bannister, who shook his head, trying to clear his thoughts.

"Where is she?" asked the lawyer.

"Over in the sheriff's office—waiting to identify the other man who kidnapped her," replied Silent.

"Other . . . man," stammered Chuck Duggan.

"That's right," nodded Silent, pushing his hat to the back of his head.

Peter saw the signal and came into the saloon, stopping between the poker table and the door. The five men all looked at him.

"Meet Peter Benson," said Silent. "He's the one who brought Debby home. He found her in a cave along Bubbling River. In the rescue process, he had to kill one of the kidnappers left there to guard her."

Silent didn't take his eyes off Chuck Duggan's back. Everyone in the room was tense, wondering what was going to take place next.

"Jack . . ." Chuck Duggan's voice trailed off as he looked across the table at Bannister, who was making faces at him to be still.

"Perhaps you should have stayed with him, Chuck," Silent said evenly.

"Me, stay with—hey, wait a minute, I ain't done n-nothin'," stammered Chuck Duggan, looking at Silent.

"No?" queried Silent. "What's that black mask sticking out of your hip pocket for—a masquerade?"

Chuck reached into his hip pocket before he realized what he was doing. He muttered a curse and kicked his chair backward, trying to hit Silent, who was prepared and sidestepped the chair. Chuck Duggan's right hand was clawing for his gun as he fell sideways. He brought up the gun. But before he could fire, a gun behind Silent roared, and Chuck Duggan's weapon clattered to the floor where he was crumpled like a sack of potatoes.

"Too slow," said Harry as he walked over, his smoking gun gripped in his right hand. "Anyone else?"

"Much obliged," said Silent, swinging back to those at the table.

Bill Hansen was out of his chair, backing up toward the bar, hands held shoulder high.

"I—I want nothin' to do with this," he said. "Count me out!"

Mike Nelson and one of his hands grabbed Bill and backed him against the bar, with the ranch hand's six-shooter boring into his side. Hansen cringed, his eyes wide with fear.

"I had nothin' to do with all this," he said.

"Perhaps not, but in some ways you were involved," said Silent. "I have a lot of proof that can send a bunch of people to prison for a long, long time."

"Bosh!" grunted Bannister. "You can't scare me."

"I'm not here to scare anyone, Mr. Bannister," said Silent. "If the truth scares you, it's too bad."

Silent stepped over and picked Chuck Duggan's gun up from the floor and looked at it.

"It could be the gun used for murder," he said. "We'll check it."

Silent looked at the three men left at the table. Then he pushed young Duggan's gun inside the waistband of his Levi's and pulled a piece of paper from his hip pocket. He smoothed it out and looked directly at Bannister.

"This will interest all present," Silent said. "And it

will shock some who thought it wasn't in existence. This is the will of Jim Benson."

"You're lying!" snapped Bannister. "Unless you stole it from my office."

"Listen and see if I took it from your office—or if it came from some other place," said Silent. Then he read:

" 'This is my last will and testament. I am of sound mind and in good health, but I want to write it now to prevent any trouble after I die. As my witness, Neal Thompson will verify that I have all my faculties.

" 'I hereby leave all my interests: the Box B ranch, my interest in the Golden Eagle Mine, the Flat Bottom Hotel, the general store, and the Silver Coin Saloon plus all my money in the local bank to my only living relative, Peter Benson of—"

"Oh, no!" exclaimed Thompson, looking sharply at Bannister, who just sat there, his face as white as a sheet.

"I—I . . ." Bannister's words failed him as Silent laughed.

"Yes, you thought you destroyed the original will," nodded Silent. "But first you copied it word for word until it came to Peter's name. You substituted Annie's name. I have the fake will in my possession, the one that gives Annie everything. I also have a letter from Annie saying she would be glad to help you in your big deal."

Bannister swallowed hard as he glanced from Clyde Duggan to Thompson. Then he sat there, all eyes upon him. Suddenly he muttered a curse and pushed the table away from him, knocking Clyde Duggan backward, almost into Silent. Silent moved quickly to avoid the chair with Duggan, and in that instant, Bannister drew a gun from his trouser waistband. But before he could level it, Silent had his own gun out and was firing.

Bannister's bullet plowed into the wooden floor as he grabbed at his midsection. He looked down to see blood seep through his fingers.

"Damn you!" he snarled at Silent. "You broke into my office!"

"I unlocked the door," said Silent. "I don't know who ransacked your office, but I believe it was Jack Harris. I knew you wanted the Box B ranch so you could sell it to Bill Hansen—or at least an interest in it."

"How'd you know that?" asked Hansen.

"I found some interesting letters in Bannister's desk drawers," replied Silent, looking directly at the lawyer. "There's gold on the Box B, isn't there?"

"How'd you know?" asked Bannister weakly.

"Jim Benson wrote Peter about it," said Silent.

Peter nodded his head as Bannister squinted at him.

"I wished they'd have killed you!" Bannister told Silent.

"Too bad to disappoint you," said Silent. "I spotted Jack Harris and his silver ring as one of the two men who came to our hotel room. I'm sure he hit me on the head and killed old Barney."

"Guessing," grunted Bannister.

"Maybe, but I think I hit the mark," said Silent. "That gold on the Box B could be more valuable than the Golden Eagle, and Bill Hansen wanted it so he could get even with his brother for old wounds. Now, why were Charley King and Fred Hansen really murdered?"

No one would speak, so he took another shot in the dark.

"One of the Double D held up the stage, while the others killed these two men. They tried to make it look like someone was after the payroll, but they actually wanted these two men out of the way. And if Jim Benson hadn't died, they would have killed him. That left Thompson in charge of everything at the mine. Bannister, you never notified the relatives of the two dead men that they would receive their shares in the Golden Eagle Mine. You were going to cover it up and make it look like these relatives sold their shares to Thompson, and you, Bannister, would then get a share."

"You're just guessin'," snorted Thompson. "It's all lies!"

"Is it?" queried Silent. "I can prove it all. Bannister was a terrible lawyer because he never covered up his trail. He left proof of everything in his desk."

"That's a blasted lie!" hissed Bannister as he slid out of his chair and landed on the floor.

Suddenly Clyde Duggan whirled out of his chair, sending it backward in an attempt to hit Silent, while he drew his gun from his holster. Silent sidestepped the chair and went for his own gun. But another gun behind him blasted out and Duggan grabbed at his chest, spun around, and went down to the floor. His gun fell at Silent's feet. The tall cowboy picked up the gun and turned to see Peter Benson standing there, a smoking weapon in his right hand.

"Thanks, Pete," he said, then turned back and looked

at Thompson. "You seem to be the only one left, left to face a long prison term."

"It was all Bannister's idea," Thompson said weakly. "He planned it all when he found out about the gold on the Box B ranch. He wanted to combine the ranch and the mine—and have a big share for himself."

"You helped him," said Silent. "You might as well confess. You know, confession's good for the soul."

"I haven't a thing to add to what you said," said Thompson, shaking his head. "I don't know how you did it."

"It wasn't easy," said Silent. "Do you know who killed Benson, King, and Hansen?"

"It was between Chuck Duggan and Jack Harris," Thompson replied. "I don't know which one killed who, but I know they did all the killing."

"Then this gun was used for murder," grunted Silent, examining Chuck's weapon.

The sheriff moved in beside Thompson and clamped handcuffs on his wrists just as Doc Schulte came bustling into the saloon with his medicine bag. He looked at the Duggans, shook his head, and went to Bannister.

"Pretty bad, Doc?" asked Bannister.

After a brief examination, Doc nodded.

"It is, Bannister. I don't see how you've lived as long as you have."

"What are you going to do about Annie?" asked Bannister, looking at Silent.

"I doubt if we need her," said Silent. "If she'll just pull out, I'm sure the law will forget her part in this deal."

The sheriff nodded. "We've got what we want. She can go."

"Good," grunted Bannister. "She—she was going crazy. Claimed she talked with Jim Benson's ghost." He shook his head and closed his eyes.

"She might have been right, Clay," said a voice behind Bannister.

The lawyer opened his eyes and looked around behind him. "Who was that?" he asked anxiously.

"Jim Benson—don't you recognize my voice, Clay?"

Bannister shook his head wearily and looked at Silent.

"Very clever, Slade," he muttered. "But I won't buy it from you like she did. Benson never called me Clay. It was always Bannister." He chuckled and toppled over on his right side.

Doc quickly moved in and checked him. Then he looked up at Silent and shook his head.

"Three dead," he said.

"Four," corrected Silent. "Jack Harris is out by the cave. We'll have to get him in the morning." He turned and looked at Thompson. "Didn't work out like you had planned, did it?"

Neal Thompson shook his head and sighed deeply.

"Like I said before, I don't know how you did it, Slade, but you had it all pretty well worked out."

"There's one thing. Whatever happened to the horses that King and Hansen were riding?" asked Silent.

"The boys brought them back to the mine," replied Thompson. "An' to think, Bannister thought we had the world by the tail."

"The tail slipped," said Silent. "It always does. That old saying is true: crime doesn't pay."

The sheriff took Thompson by the arm and walked him past Silent and Irish, who moved in next to his partner.

"Shall I tell Annie that she's free to go now?" asked Wilbur.

"You better," nodded Silent. "Let her take the stage in the morning."

Wilbur Wendell nodded as he herded Thompson out of the saloon, followed by Harry Baylor.

Peter Benson came up beside Silent, a wide grin on his tired face.

"Gee, I don't know how you did it, but you did," he said. "Where'd you find that will?"

Silent looked around, then leaned forward and whispered to Peter:

"I wrote it," he said softly. "I guess I can change things if a lawyer thinks he can. But I believe what I wrote is the way the original was, Pete. Bannister never said it wasn't."

"But my uncle's signature on it?" queried Peter.

"I did what Bannister did. I copied it from one of your uncle's letters," grinned Silent. "Anyway, it's all over and you're in charge of all of your uncle's properties."

"I just can't believe it," said Peter. "Just yesterday I was riding away from everything here. Now I'm back."

"And so is Debby," said Irish.

"Oh, my gosh!" gasped Peter. He grabbed Silent's

right hand and pumped it, then turned and ran out of the saloon.

Mike Nelson came up to Silent, offering his hand. His tired, wrinkled face was all smiles.

"I dunno what to say," Mike said. "It's like a bad nightmare."

"That's just what it was," said Silent. "You better check on those young ones. They're going to need a little help getting their lives straightened out."

"I'll help, but I know what's goin' to happen, Slade." The rancher paused and looked closely at Silent. "Will you be the best man?"

"That all depends on when," laughed Silent as Nelson walked out of the saloon.

Irish looked at Silent. "You don't plan on staying here, do you?"

"No," replied Silent.

"Then why agree to be the best man?"

"I told Mike it all depends on when," said Silent. "We came here, took care of what we were asked to do, and now we're free to pull out any time we want to—wedding or not."

Just then Bill Hansen came up to Silent and Irish. He looked the tall cowboy in the eyes.

"I don't know what to say," he said slowly, shaking his head. "I didn't know it was this bad down here, and all because I wanted the Box B."

"You'll probably have a share of your brother's interest in the Golden Eagle as soon as that's all straightened out," said Silent.

Hansen nodded. "I shouldn't take it," he said. "We hated each other from childhood. Always fighting. Maybe I'll give my share to my sister. I think I could live with myself then." He paused and shook his head. "I never thought Bannister would go to such means to gain that ranch. I wanted everything legal."

"Is it that valuable?" queried Silent.

"I believe it is," nodded Hansen. "The ore we got from out in the hills to the north of the ranch house was very, very rich. I guess it was worth it to Bannister."

He turned and walked out of the saloon. Silent watched him, then looked at Irish, who was grinning.

"What's so funny?"

"The way things worked out, just like I thought they would," Irish replied.

"Yeah? That's interesting," said Silent. "I'm just glad it's all over."

"Well, we didn't see Jim Benson, but we took care of what seemed to be troublin' him," said Irish.

"That's good," grunted Silent.

"Do you think Benson didn't trust Bannister?" asked Irish.

Silent nodded. "I think he found out too late, though. Well, let's see how the young couple are doing."